"You're Amy Parker, right?"

"Yes."

"Then this is for you," the waiter said, handing her a long-stemmed red rose and a small white envelope.

With a little laugh, she opened the letter and read its message by the light of the candle.

You are the most beautiful girl here. I have been across the room watching you. If you want to see who I am, look into the spotlight at the end of this song.

Stunned, Amy blinked her eyes. She didn't know how to react. Was this for real? If so, who could possibly have sent it? She was just breathing in the rose's perfume when the song ended. Amy followed the spotlight.

She saw him immediately. There he stood, gazing at her and smiling. His blond hair glistened. He wore an old-fashioned white tuxedo jacket and baggy slacks. As he slowly walked toward her, the light seemed to stick to him, and everything else faded into nothingness. But Amy still couldn't believe her eyes.

It was Cole Stewart.

FAWCETT GIRLS ONLY BOOKS

Sunset High

SUNSET HIGH

SWEPT AWAY

Linda A. Cooney

FAWCETT GIRLS ONLY • NEW YORK

RLI:
VL: Grades 6 + up

IL: Grades 7 + up

1

AMY PARKER WRIGGLED IN HER CHAIR AND WONDERED JUST how much longer she'd have to wait. She'd been there an hour already. Her mother had dropped her at the Minneapolis airport and then hustled her little sister off to summer school. When her mom had worried about making Amy wait by herself for her plane to Los Angeles, Amy'd made it clear that she didn't mind a bit. Better to be alone, she'd thought to herself. Airports are so romantic.

"Romantic, pfffff," Amy puffed now.

What was romantic about hard-backed plastic chairs, an airplane that was delayed, and having to wait forever to get where you were dying to go? Nothing. Oh, sure, in the movies and on soap operas and stuff airports were the places where people had passionate reunions and tearful good-byes, but the only reunion Amy had witnessed so far was of a three-year-old boy and his grandmother. It was sweet but hardly romantic. Especially when he'd started wailing and pounding his plastic car on his grandmother's head.

Amy sighed, hooked her thumbs in her suspenders, and stretched her knickered legs a little farther out over her suitcase. She rubbed the back of her neck, just under her dark blond hair, and stared up into the white perforated ceiling tiles. If she had to wait much longer, she was going to jump out of her skin.

"Just calm down. Getting crazed won't make the plane leave any sooner," she told herself.

Don't get excited, flustered, wild, or carried away. That was her father's favorite way to describe her—carried away. "Amy, don't get carried away," her father had warned her that morning. He'd said it with a little grin, and Amy knew what he'd been referring to. She almost told him it would be good if he got carried away every once in a while.

But as much as Amy hated to admit it, her father had a point. Sometimes she *did* truly get carried away. But not this time. This time there wasn't really anything to worry about. Most often when Amy went truly out of control, it was over some incredibly handsome guy. "Some weirdo," as her father said, just because some of them were a little unusual ... had an earring, or a first name like Lars, or an old, old pickup truck. She would call those guys special, unique . . . not weird.

But the object of this trip had nothing to do with guys, weird or otherwise. Amy was going to Beverly Hills to see her best friend, Kristin Sullivan—"Legs," as Amy called her. Kristin had moved West that spring, and Amy couldn't wait to see her again. Even so, her father had been reluctant to give his permission to let Amy take this trip. After all, she was going to Hollywood, and wasn't Hollywood the place where crazy things happened?

But in the end Amy had won out. She had assured her father that *nothing* crazy or weird or out-of-control could happen on this trip. No way. First, she had promised. Second, she was going to Hollywood to see Kristin, and while offhand that might sound exotic, Amy knew that her friend was the most practical girl in the world. Even her father knew it, and it was one of the reasons he'd agreed that she could go.

Now Amy was so excited she wanted to bubble over. There were a million things to talk about with Kristin, and it was like a dream going to the West Coast, but the romantic, wide-eyed, try-it-and-see Amy would have to keep it together. That is, if her dumb plane would ever get it together to take off and fly her there.

Amy looked at her watch and shook her head. "One-thirty," she considered. Since the end of school, one-thirty had become the time of day for watching *Reflections,* the soap opera that she and her friends had gotten hooked on since Kristin'd written to say she was friends with a girl named Monica Miller who actually acted on the show. It wasn't a bad soap, and Amy had ambitions to be a writer. She liked to try to guess where the plot would go. If they would at least let her on board, she might be able to watch it on the big screen where they projected television shows until the plane took off.

Suddenly Amy sat up and brushed back a strand of wheat-blond hair. Of course, that's what those ugly black chairs were across from her: pay-television sets. You put in a quarter and sat there and watched for fifteen minutes. They were mildly corny, and they looked like something out of *The Twilight Zone,* but for a quarter ...

Amy dragged her luggage over and immediately sat down. Just in time she produced a coin and slipped it in. She switched the channel and heard the theme music coming up.

"Now that's better," she whispered.

At least she was doing something more interesting than just waiting. A character named Felicia was on. She was about Amy's age and very beautiful. This gorgeous young British actor played opposite Felicia, some guy named Cole Stewart. He was slim and blond, square-jawed, with these sexy brown eyes—definitely not the type ever seen at Ontario High. Most of Amy's friends were

4

wild about Cole, and Amy couldn't say she blamed them.

Amy strained to hear the dialogue as Cole passionately embraced Felicia, but there was so much activity going on in the airport that it wasn't easy. She cupped her hands over her ears to try to block out the noise behind her. Still, she could barely hear the show. Cole had just kissed Felicia and was saying something. Amy could tell it was important. She turned her head, almost shushing the crowd behind her, when another sound filtered into her excited brain....

LAST CALL FOR FLIGHT 509 TO LOS ANGELES. LAST CALL FOR FLIGHT 509 TO LOS ANGELES.

"Oh my God!" Amy gasped.

A boy sitting next to her at another pay-TV booth looked up with startled eyes.

"That's my plane!"

Amy was running now, full speed. Her stomach felt as if it had shrunk to the size of a little stone, and she could feel the cold sweat running down her back. People were ducking out of her way as she sprinted by, clutching her suitcase under her arm like a football. Like a maniac she scrambled and wove her way to the departure gate.

"Did I miss the plane to L.A.?" she panted, getting there just as an attendant was closing the door.

The woman shook her head and let Amy through. "You just made it," she scolded.

Amy handed in her ticket and gave her brow a wipe. "Thanks," she sighed.

Amy made her way to her seat and sat down after shoving her bag in the bin overhead. She was suddenly exhausted, and her heart was still in her throat. What if she had missed her plane? That would have been a disaster! She sat back and looked out the window, shaking her head. "No more craziness," she said under her breath. "Everything has to stay calm."

But as the big airliner began to speed down the runway, Amy somehow knew that calm wasn't the way it was going to be.

Most people in the Los Angeles airport looked either excited to be headed off on some exotic voyage or exhausted to be returning from one. Then there were some people who were neither excited nor exhausted: business people doing business, travelers making connections, soldiers going back to base. Denis Daniels wasn't sure where he belonged. When he tried to figure it out, it made his head hurt. Was he a child being sent off to boarding school or a criminal on his way to jail?

"Have you ever been to Hawaii before?"

Denis Daniels looked at the clerk behind the airport counter and grimly shook his head.

"Oh, you'll love it."

Denis silently kicked his duffel bag but didn't say a word. You'll love it. What a joke. As if he was flying to Hawaii for some kind of paradise vacation. Ha-ha.

Denis's father's voice burst through the automatic doors. "Denis! Just go in the first-class line. Just go up to the front."

Denis cringed. That was like his dad to run in after parking the car, not even take a look around, but assume that Denis was eligible for every privilege. Just because he was a rich network executive and his wife was a famous TV star, Mr. Daniels thought Denis should act and be treated like boy wonder. Instead, Denis acted like boy screw-up. Flicking his golden hair away from his eyes, Denis moved up. At least if he couldn't stay in public school in California, he could stand with everybody else in the coach line for his flight to Hawaii.

"Did you hear me?" Mr. Daniels asked.

"Keep cool, Dad. There's no rush. We're really early."

Mr. Daniels didn't push it. At least they had made some progress from those weeks of family therapy up in Marin County. Now Denis was headed to some program for troubled kids in Hawaii. Because of his problems with drugs and alcohol— and then totaling his Porsche up on Mulholland Boulevard—the therapist said the place in Hawaii was what he needed. Denis knew he needed something. He just hoped this place in Hawaii wasn't like some kind of reform school.

"Your mother would've come if she hadn't had

that taping today," Mr. Daniels said, looking off in the other direction. "You know she loves you."

Denis shrugged. He was glad his mother wasn't there. He hated people staring, coming up asking for her autograph. Besides, his mom was so emotional, either disgustingly cheery or weepy as a waterfall. Denis hated good-byes. He hated emotions. Right now he didn't want to feel anything.

When they reached the front of the line, Denis tossed his duffel bag and the four other suitcases onto the metal shelf. He could tell what the check-in lady was thinking: it was an awful lot of luggage for an island vacation. Denis couldn't look her in the eye. Finally it was all taken care of, and they began to walk toward the gate.

"You work things out, you'll be back by fall," his father said.

"Yeah." Denis didn't want to think about it.

"I don't think you'll lose your driver's license," Mr. Daniels continued. "My lawyer's been working on it. When you come back, we'll see about getting you a car again, but believe me, this time it's not going to be a Porsche."

Denis looked out the window to the airplane that would soon be taking him away from his parents, away from Sunset High, to a place where "problem" teenagers were supposed to be straightened out. It was bad enough he had to think about going to that place, but his father bringing up memories of the accident . . .

Denis put his hand to his eyes as a vision of his

totaled Porsche came back to him. It was upside-down and burning; even now Denis could smell the fumes.

"The guy who runs this place has had great success with kids like you," his father was saying. "He's tough, but he's fair. If you get in . . ."

Denis wasn't listening. He'd suddenly seen a familiar figure walking toward him down the corridor of the airport. When she finally looked up and spotted him staring, the numbness went away and all the feeling came rushing back.

"Denis!"

"Kristin."

Denis stared at Kristin Sullivan's lovely freckled face, clear green eyes, and long sandy brown hair. She smiled. He wanted to hold her, press his face to hers, but he knew he couldn't. Her boyfriend, Grady, stood right next to her, and besides, it would make him feel too much.

For once Denis's father showed some sensitivity. He knew that Denis wanted to be left alone. "Give me your ticket, Den. I'll go get you a seat."

"Thanks."

"Denis, where are you going?" asked Grady. His gaze was friendly. There was no sense of jealousy or resentment, which was amazing, considering that Denis had been in love with Kristin. Of course, Kristin had always been in love with Grady, so what was there to be jealous about?

Denis tried to slough it off. "Hawaii. Some fancy school. Screw-up surf camp."

Neither Kristin nor Grady laughed. She knew that he was going away; Denis had written and told her.

"How about you?" Denis tried to joke. "You two stealing off to Italy on your dad's American Express card?"

Kristin smiled. "I'm meeting my best friend from Minnesota. She's supposed to be coming in any minute."

Denis put his hands on the waistband of his Levi's and took a step back. "I guess you'd better go, then. You don't want to miss her." He was glad for an excuse to leave them. He knew where things stood with Kristin. There was no need to go through it again.

She looked into his face with the superdirect stare of hers and touched his hand. "Okay." She hesitated. "Everybody's going to miss you."

Denis looked away. This was just the kind of sentimentality he wanted to avoid. He looked down as if there were something fascinating written on the floor.

Kristin wouldn't quite leave yet. "Denis?"

"Yeah."

"Have you talked to JT? Is she okay?"

At the mention of JT the blood rushed to Denis's head, and he almost had to sit down. This was what he really wanted to avoid. Seeing Kristin was rough, but he knew where things stood and it was over. He could handle it. But JT was another story. JT had shared the final unlucky ride in his Porsche. When he thought about how JT loved him, he was overwhelmed with a million conflicting feelings that he couldn't begin to understand.

"I don't know," Denis finally answered. "Have you talked to her?"

Kristin shook her head. "I don't know her very well. I just think the whole thing was probably hard for her. I'm sure she'd like to know that you're going away."

Denis stuck his hands in his pockets and slouched, almost as though he were trying to keep anything from getting too close. He knew he should call JT and say good-bye. He *wanted* to call her. He liked her; maybe he even loved her. But he didn't love her the way she loved him. He never would. So what was he supposed to say when he called ... I'm sorry I can't love you: I'm sorry I almost got you killed. I'm not worthy of you, anyway. I'm sorry, I'm sorry, I'm sorry. . . .

Saying good-bye to JT would mean admitting everything about himself that was worthless and hollow, uncaring and without hope. JT was Denis's deepest wound, and he was afraid the pain of opening it up would drive him crazy.

"Denis, do you know when you'll be back?" he heard Kristin ask.

"Soon." He tried to smile and put up a good front. He could tell that Kristin saw right through it.

"Take care of yourself. Write to me."

"Take care, Den," Grady added.

Denis backed up and waved. He even made his legs bounce and forced a carefree look. No sense in not going out in style.

"I'll send you postcards ... and reports on the native girls."

Kristin and Grady watched him.

If Denis had been wearing a hat, he would have tipped it. Since he wasn't, he just turned and quickly walked away.

❀ 2

KRISTIN!!!!!

AAAMMYYYYY!!!!

AAAAAAAAHHHHHHHH!!!!!!

Tears ran down Amy's cheeks as she threw her arms around her best friend. She wasn't sure why she was crying, but as soon as she spotted Kristin's lanky frame and her freckled face, Amy's feelings just went crazy. She wanted to jump up and down and laugh, but instead she started to weep. But that was okay. Amy knew that emotions were like floods or tornadoes—when they hit, there was no point in resisting.

The girls backed up to look at each other. Grinning and dry-eyed, Kristin hugged Amy one more time. "Why are you crying?" She laughed.

Amy tried to look indignant. "Well, why do you think, Legs?" She sniffled. "I miss you so much."

"I miss you, too." Kristin held her shoulders. "You look exactly the same."

Amy paused. They had not seen each other in over five months, and she knew Kristin was right. Her hair was still the same combination of wheat and blond, thick and layered to her shoulders. Her skin was still rosy, her figure compact and curvy. Even her paisley suspenders were the ones that Kristin's family had given her for her seventeenth birthday.

But Kristin. Kristin was another story....

Amy held her best friend's hands and looked into her face for a second, not letting Kristin move away. Kristin had definitely changed. It wasn't the kind of change kids had gossiped about back in St. Cloud. Kristin hadn't bleached her hair or gone punk. Maybe her clothes were a little softer, her complexion not quite so pale ... still nothing drastic or overwhelming. But after a second of looking, Amy thought she knew. It was her eyes. Kristin's warm green eyes looked different: warmer, greener, happier.

"Come meet Grady," Kristin said.

"I can't wait."

Amy let Kristin lead her over to the waiting area. A dark-haired boy bobbed up before he even saw her. He was as leggy as Kristin, and his face was open, his eyes full of expectation. It had to be Grady.

14

He picked up Amy's bag, slung it over his shoulder, and put his other arm around Kristin. Kristin snuggled against him.

"Hi," he said to Amy. His eyes were an intense blue. "I feel like I know you already."

Amy blushed. The electricity between Grady and Kristin gave her goose bumps. "Me, too." She gulped.

"Welcome to L.A." He smiled and pulled a pair of sunglasses out of his multipocketed vest. "Why don't you two go down and pick up the luggage. I'll get the jeep."

"Okay."

Amy watched him take off through the airport in a slow, graceful run. After he'd disappeared into the crowd, Amy nudged Kristin with her elbow. "Not bad," she teased. "He's not quite as cute as Worm Reinheart, but he'll do."

They both started to laugh. Worm—whose real name was Ward—was a boy from their fourth-grade class who had adored Kristin and brought her dead bugs as presents.

"It took me a long time to get over Worm," Kristin came back, "but I finally decided it was time to stop pining away for spiders and ants and go for Grady instead."

Amy hugged Kristin again. Even after their being separated, Amy felt that they could begin right where they had left off. No awkwardness or having to start over. It was as if they had seen each other yesterday.

"Well, what's new in St. Cloud?"

"I have hellos for you from about a hundred thousand people."

"I want to hear how everybody is. Let's go get your stuff first."

"Okay."

Buzzing with energy, Amy wove through the crowded airport. She looked for telltale signs that she was in an exotic place—anything that would confirm that this was southern California, home of orange trees, weird cults, and movie stars. They were nearing the airport security check and passed an old man dressed all in purple waving a sign—something about how everybody in Los Angeles should save the animals by not wearing leather shoes.

Fascinated, Amy headed right for him, but as soon as Amy veered off course, Kristin pulled her elbow.

"This way, Parker."

"Oh, Kristin, that guy looks so interesting. Let's go talk to him."

Kristin kept right on tugging. Amy laughed. Yes, their friendship was still the same as ever. Kristin was still pulling Amy back on track—keeping her from getting in over her head—making sure that she didn't get carried away.

Amy shrugged happily and followed. The guy did look a little too weird; besides, there would be lots of time to soak up Los Angeles atmosphere. They went down into the baggage area. Being a good reporter, as they walked Amy kept her eyes peeled. They passed older ladies with overly tanned skin and tight blouses, a group of guys who looked like a New Wave band, and a huge woman who Amy suspected was really a man. Wow, Amy thought, the purple man was just the beginning. There were so many amazing people here. She couldn't help imagining where they all lived and what their lives were like. Maybe she should interview one of them for her school paper. Eyes wide with curiosity, Amy made a full circle, ending up face-to-face with Kristin's level, straightforward stare.

"So really, how's everybody back home?" Kristin asked, a touch of homesickness in her voice.

Amy tried to forget about all the interesting characters and watched for her luggage as the conveyer rumbled and began to turn. "Good," she told Kristin. "The cheerleading squad was never as good after you left, but we all knew that was going to happen. I brought you the yearbook and a bunch of letters and pictures from our junior picnic. They're in my suitcase. How about you? How're your folks?"

"A lot better," Kristin said brightly.

Kristin had written Amy all about the rough time her parents had been through. Things had seemed as if they were getting really bad for a while, and Kristin had worried that her parents were breaking up. In the end that turned out not to be true at all; but it had affected Kristin's relationship with Grady, and there was a period where they hadn't even been talking. That was the worst, but Kristin had learned a painful lesson about not keeping everything pent up inside. Kristin was just the opposite of Amy. Amy was the last person to try to hold her feelings back.

"What about the guy who's Deann Daniels's son?" Amy asked, craning to look down the snaky conveyer belt.

"Denis?"

"Yeah. You know, I read an article about him on the plane," Amy said more softly. She smiled. "I can't believe conservative Kristin Sullivan got to know him. He sounded so wild."

"It's just a good thing you weren't here," Kristin came back. "You would've encouraged him."

Amy gave Kristin a little nudge, and they wrapped their arms together. Springing to her tiptoes, Amy spotted her large suitcase. It had come open on one side, and her old riding jodphurs were bursting out. Leaping onto the carousel, Amy teetered, pulled the case down, then jumped off, almost plowing into a Japanese tourist.

Kristin helped her drag it away from the crowd. After relocking the clasp, both girls sat on it. "It's weird. I just ran into Denis here before we met you. I hadn't seen him since he crashed his car."

Amy nodded and looked concerned.

"He's going to some special place in Hawaii for

kids with problems." Kristin paused. "He's going to be okay, I hope."

Just then Grady jogged up. "Let's go," he panted. "I'm illegally parked. I told the cop I was picking up a famous dignitary." Hoisting Amy's suitcase over his shoulder, he led the way out to his jeep, which was waiting at the curb.

Once through the glass doors, Amy had to stop. The insides of airports were great places for reunions and good-byes, but they never gave a good sense of the town itself. Standing outside, the light heat caressing her body, it finally hit Amy with full force that she was someplace new, someplace very different. The horizon was grayish, and the air had an odd thick smell. In front of her was a parking lot that went on forever, filled with what looked like an army of cars. In the distance was a control tower high as a skyscraper—a lot bigger than a St. Cloud grain elevator.

"Wake up, Amy, time to go," Kristin reminded her. She was standing at the open door of the old white jeep. Amy climbed in, seat springs creaking, and the jeep bumped into the chaotic airport traffic. Pitched forward, leaning between the two front seats, Amy couldn't stop beaming. She was embarking on the adventure of a lifetime.

Grady looked at her in the rearview mirror. "I hope you're not tired. We're meeting a bunch of people in Westwood to see the new *Star Wars* movie tonight."

Amy and Kristin smiled at each other. "Amy never gets tired," Kristin told Grady.

"Good." Grady laughed. "The line will probably wind around the block three times. Maybe Amy will keep the rest of us awake."

"You mean I get to meet everybody tonight?" Amy marveled. She had heard so much about Kristin's new friends—Eddie and Elena Santiago, Holly Harris, Josh Ross, and Monica Miller. Amy had a clear image of every single one and couldn't wait to meet them. "They all sound so great."

Grady laughed. "I hope you still say that two weeks from now. You'll be seeing a lot of them." He and Kristin smiled at each other, a funny kind of smile, as if they were holding something back.

"Really?" Amy knew Kristin would never hide her in the closet, but she'd been a little afraid that some of the kids would be away for the summer. It would have been awful to miss Eddie the comedian, his girlfriend, Holly Harris, or his sister Elena the fitness nut, and most of all Monica the soap opera star. Amy even had an idea for a short story about a group of friends in Hollywood. Maybe she would make it into a screenplay.

"We have a full schedule set up for you," Kristin grinned. "I know how you hate being busy."

Amy bounced on the seat. "I *did* bring *Wuthering Heights* to reread for the tenth time and two empty journals to fill, just in case things got dull."

"Well, you can write in the mornings when I'm

working at the restaurant. Other than that, I don't think you'll have to worry about being bored."

"I'm never bored," Amy tossed back. It was true. Even in routine St. Cloud, she always found something new and intriguing—but here ... here the possibilities could go on forever.

Again Kristin and Grady smiled at each other in a funny way that sent a tingle down Amy's spine. Could they have something really special planned for her? As soon as the idea entered Amy's head, the words were flying out of her mouth. "What! Tell me what!"

Kristin and Grady laughed. Amy took off her white jockey cap and slapped it against Kristin's shoulder.

"Be patient. We'll tell you," Kristin cautioned. "First, we want to take you to this new disco called The Pink Whale—it's the hot new place, and we haven't even been there yet. Then there's this Renaissance Fair thing we're all going to. That's this coming weekend."

"What's a Renaissance Fair?"

Kristin laughed. "Beats me. It's something Eddie and Elena go to every year. I guess it's some kind of old-fashioned street fair: sort of with knights and ladies and wandering minstrels ... stuff like that."

The Renaissance. That was the period of Romeo and Juliet ... palaces, court jesters, royalty. Amy could hardly imagine anything better than making a fair around a Renaissance theme. She rested her chin on Kristin's shoulder. "And back home all we have are prize pigs."

Kristin turned around, and both girls burst into laughter at a shared memory. "Don't remind me!"

For Amy it quickly bubbled into that I'll-never-stop-laughing feeling. She loved that silly kind of giddiness and knew how easy it was to get Kristin into the same state.

Grady gave them a left-out look. "What's so funny?"

"Last year Kristin and I went to the state fair together," Amy managed.

"Oh, no! Don't tell him." Kristin giggled, covering her face.

Amy couldn't resist. "No more secrets, Sullivan." Leaning all the way forward, she took a short, excited breath. "Willie Nelson was playing there, and I wanted to get this interview of him for my school paper. So I met this guy who was one of his roadies." Amy nudged Kristin. "Remember how handsome he was?"

Kristin nodded. "He was. But he was weird, too. Remember his hair? It was almost to his waist."

"He called himself Mountain Boy." Amy fell back against the backseat, a hand over her plaid shirt. "But he was incredibly gorgeous."

Both girls laughed again, this time even louder.

Amy's eyes were starting to tear over. "He kept calling me his country blossom, and he wrote me that awful poem."

Grady had a skeptical look on his face. "Wait a

second. I don't know if I really do want to hear this."

Kristin sucked in air, almost wheezing, she was laughing so hard. "Amy talked Mountain Boy into letting her backstage to try to see Willie Nelson...."

Amy burst in. "It was really dark, and I had to climb over this fence to get to where the dressing rooms were, and ... and ..." Amy was unable to finish, she was so out of control.

"And Amy didn't really know where she was going...."

"Which never stopped me before ..."

Both girls were now laughing so hard that Kristin's face was red and Amy was fanning herself with her hand, making infectious hooting noises. Just listening to them laugh made Grady crack up.

"So what happened?"

Kristin caught her breath. "So Amy climbed over the fence and slipped and fell...." Kristin couldn't finish. She was gone again.

Amy took over. "I fell into this pen with about a hundred little piglets, baby pigs. They were all snorting and screaming and jumping on each other's backs. It was like some out-of-control cartoon. I started yelling, but every time I yelled, the pigs just squealed louder...."

"Then I came back after her, because I was afraid Mountain Boy had just told her to go back there so he could jump her bones or something, and I climbed up and ..."

"AND FELL IN TOO!!!" both girls shouted at the same time.

Grady pulled off the freeway, the jeep circling down a spiral ramp. When he stopped at the light on Wilshire, he rested his elbow on the steering wheel and waited for the two of them to calm down. Finally they slowed to a manic pant, and he smiled and shook his head.

"It's taken me five months to semicivilize this girl," he teased Amy, looking back at Kristin. "Why do I feel like having you here is going to be a big step backward?"

"I'm always a terrible influence." Amy grinned, her arms on the back of the seat. "At least I hope I am."

Finally Kristin was almost calm. She turned back to Amy and pointed a finger. "I don't believe this. I haven't even told you the main thing we have planned for you, and you've already gotten me totally off on a tangent."

"You mean you have more planned?" Amy stared out the window as they lurched through Westwood. Overhead huge glass office buildings reflected the late-afternoon sun and tall palm trees shimmied. She felt that if she slipped out the jeep window, she might just float to the top of one of those palms and wiggle there, too.

"There's definitely more," Grady enticed.

"Ooh, tell me."

Kristin swiveled around and stifled another laugh.

"There's a party next week in Malibu, at Monica's uncle's beach house."

"I'm invited?"

"No. I told you about it because you have to stay home." She giggled. "Of course you're invited."

A party at the house of a soap star! Amy could hardly believe it! Sandy beaches, wooden decks, gorgeous suntanned guys. She was almost breathless. "You mean Monica really wants me to come?" The character Monica played on the soap seemed so sweet and vulnerable; still Amy wondered if in person the actress would be supercool. But she also figured any good friend of Kristin's could never be too standoffish.

"Not only that," Kristin continued.

They held on as Grady made a hard turn, pulling off the busy boulevard and onto a narrow residential street. The houses were huge, many hidden behind lush hedges and elaborate gates.

"The best part is that I told Monica all about you: how you're the best writer on the school paper back home and ..."

Stalled at the stop sign, Grady turned back to check her reaction. Amy felt as if she were being presented with some extravagant surprise. Kristin and Grady were waiting for her to open it. "And?"

"And Monica arranged for you to come down to the soap studio and spend a whole day watching the taping so you can write an article about it!"

"You're kidding."

25

Kristin grinned. "She's even trying to arrange for you to interview one of the cast."

"When?"

"Tomorrow. We don't mess around here. You'll have to get up at five, but we figured you wouldn't mind."

"You're not kidding."

"Nope."

Amy wanted to scream, but she was speechless. Her mouth fell open, and her heart started jumping around in her chest. Now it was Grady's turn to laugh. When the jeep rumbled on and Kristin kept that coy grin, Amy knew it was for real! A Renaissance Fair, Hollywood disco, a Malibu beach party, and ... Amy *really* could not believe it—tomorrow she was going to watch the taping of a real live soap opera! She was silent until at last they pulled up in front of a wood-and-brick two-story house with the familiar Sullivan station wagon parked in front.

Kristin and Grady hopped out, but Amy was immobile. Her legs wouldn't quite move, and she still felt as if she had been zapped with a stun gun. Finally she staggered out as Grady was lifting her bag onto the sidewalk.

"You aren't making it up, are you? About this soap opera thing?" Amy had to make sure. Sometimes her desire or her imagination fooled her into thinking things were what she wanted them to be rather than what they were.

Kristin put her long arms around her. "Would I

do that to an old friend?" They looked at each other ... two Minnesota girls a long way from home. "Welcome to Hollywood."

Amy put a hand to her heart as Kristin and Grady took an elbow on either side and led her into the house.

3

Janet Terry Gantner put her hands to her waist and squeezed. An inch of softness pressed over her index fingers. She turned her palms flat and tried to push her flesh back against the bone. It didn't work. How could it? JT had gained five pounds.

But sitting in the waiting area of Rodeo Perfect Nail, JT doubted she would ever want to eat again. The smell of nail polish was overpowering, and her stomach was already unstable with anger. Tugging on her single long earring, JT gave an irritable fluff to her short blond hair and picked up the latest copy of *Los Angeles* magazine.

"I should just leave right now," she muttered under her breath. Still she sat. With a one-handed slap, she opened the magazine's cover.

From where she was sitting, she could just

catch the arch of Nadia Lawrence's tanned foot. Just seeing the expensive Italian sandal—the maddening calm with which that foot made slow lazy circles—caused JT's insides to contract into a huge fist. She checked her watch. Nadia had been keeping her waiting for thirty-five minutes.

The foot touched linoleum, and Nadia's full form came into view. From her long reddish hair to her fashion-model face to her streamlined hips, she looked unruffled and smug.

"JT?" she called, innocent as dawn.

JT looked up.

Nadia smiled and fluttered her wet fingernails. "I just have to wait till I'm dry enough for a topcoat. You don't mind, do you?"

JT felt the outside of her mouth curve up. It was an old reflex, and JT was instantly ashamed of it. No longer was she going to be Nadia's puppet! She had finally cut the strings, and even though it was possible she might fall flat on her face, she had to fight the urge to reattach.

Nadia didn't even wait for her reply. She had plopped right back down, and the foot was circling again. JT gritted her teeth. Just because Nadia was the popular daughter of a famous movie producer was no reason for her to treat JT like some kind of lady-in-waiting. It was true that Nadia had transformed her from a chubby nothing to a stylish member of the top Sunset High social crowd. But JT had seen through her best friend, or rather ex–best friend. Nadia's cruelty to

29

Holly Harris had been the last straw. JT couldn't justify Nadia's meanness this time. She had finally broken away.

"Are you waiting for an appointment?" asked the middle-aged woman behind the desk.

JT shook her head and once more considered walking out. This was the first time she had seen Nadia in almost three weeks. The last time they'd been together had ended with JT telling Nadia off. "I am not your friend anymore!" JT had hollered. She could still feel the words in her throat. When she'd said them, she'd felt so free. Now, listening to the muffled chatter and the rattle of manicure carts, JT just felt empty.

Summer vacation was a terrible time to break off from your best friend. Before JT had been popular, she had never been this lonely. But now she knew what she was missing. Most of the other girls from the social crowd were still in Europe or Hawaii, so JT'd spent the last twenty days without speaking to one friend. And there was nothing going on in late July to distract her. She was allergic to the sun, so forget the beach. She'd worked a few days at one of her parents' gourmet cookie stores, read nine mystery novels ... and stuffed herself with chocolate. Involuntarily, JT's hands went to her waist again.

"One more minute," she heard Nadia call.

Just the voice made JT sweat. Nadia'd begged for this meeting to talk things over, and JT'd given in. She was lonely and curious. But now, after being so apologetic on the phone, Nadia was making a point of letting JT know who was still in charge.

"I'm sorry, JT," Nadia cooed as she finally appeared from behind the wall of manicure tables. She was holding her purse between the insides of her wrists. "They were running behind. You understand." Walking up to the front desk, Nadia pursed her lips. "JT?"

JT reluctantly padded up to meet her.

Nadia held out her bag. "Could you get my wallet out so I don't wreck my nails?" Her voice was sweet as a ripe melon. "Thanks. There's a ten in the first compartment."

JT opened Nadia's Gucci wallet and handed the bill to the woman at the desk.

"Give the change to Suzi as a tip," Nadia called. She was already on her way down the stairs, a wavy flag of red hair and white cotton.

JT took the dollar-and-a-half change and slammed it down on the manicurist's table. For a fleeting moment she checked if there was another way out of the shop. Maybe she could abandon Nadia, leave *her* waiting down on Rodeo Drive. But there was no other exit. The fist curling up again, JT headed down the stairs and met Nadia at the bottom.

Outside the traffic was heavy, and there was a strange smell in the hot air. Smoke and ash. There were always a rash of summer blazes out near the desert, and this year was particularly bad. On

TV each night there were more pictures of smoking houses and naked hills. The night before, the wind had carried the ash until it settled in a gray layer atop JT's swimming pool. For some reason JT was fascinated with the fires this year, and she took an extra-deep breath of the dry sooty air.

Nadia led her into Café Rodeo, and the charcoal scent was replaced by the aroma of fresh coffee and cinnamon.

"Order anything you want," Nadia said, getting comfortable in a canvas-backed chair. She smiled and took a menu.

JT glanced around. Everything inside Café Rodeo was so green: the plants, the crisscross wallpaper, the salads. The lushness only made JT feel more alienated. She identified more with the charred acres on the six o'clock news—unprotected, hurt, burnt-out.

"I'm not hungry," JT answered, putting the menu away. No more Nadia buying her lunch, taking her shopping, using her to satisfy Nadia's every whim.

Nadia shrugged and, when the waitress came over, asked simply for two mineral waters. Then she folded her hands and stared at her ex–best friend. Game time was over. Nadia's face was dead serious, and there was even a little fear in her brown eyes. For a long time she looked at JT, daring her ex-friend to look away. With all her might, JT stared back.

The water arrived. Nadia took a long sip.

"Well, JT," she began, "it's been three weeks since you threw that little scene. Do you realize how lucky you are that I'm still giving you a chance to apologize?"

JT closed her hands around her glass. Her mouth felt as parched as those blackened hills, and the fizzy water didn't seem to help. She did not answer.

Nadia exhaled sharply and crossed her arms. "All right. If you *really* don't want to be friends anymore; that's up to you. I just think there are a few things you should know."

JT cleared her throat. "What?"

"I know that you are mad at me because I got Holly Harris fired from that dumb salesgirl job at Camp Beverly Hills. Right?"

JT nodded. The memory of it made her feel even darker. How could she have accompanied Nadia on that vengeful trip to ruin Holly's reputation at all the boutiques on Rodeo Drive? And then to find out that Holly hadn't really shoplifted at all and that with a big lie Nadia had maliciously spoiled Holly's chances of getting a job. The worst part was she hadn't done a thing to stop it.

Nadia leaned forward and held up a polished finger. "When I spread that info about Holly stealing, I thought it was true. I still think it probably is. . . . She's such a fake."

JT stiffened and made herself look Nadia in the eye. "Even if you did think it was true at first, we both know that Holly's not a shoplifter." Nadia gave a hearty laugh. Infuriated, JT slammed down her drink. "After ruining her reputation like that, the least you could have done was help her get another job."

Nadia tossed back her long hair. "I didn't have to do that," she threatened, "because someone else beat me to it." A long pause. "Didn't she?"

JT shifted nervously.

"Could you have had anything to do with the fact that Holly is now working for Mrs. Gantner's Cookies?"

JT wasn't sure why she felt so defensive. She was proud of having maneuvered Holly into a job at her parents' store. Still, no one knew that she was responsible for Holly's job or why she had gone out of her way to arrange it. "Maybe I did," she mumbled.

Nadia sneered. "Yeah. I figured that."

"So what's wrong with it?"

Nadia's mouth turned into a red line of condescension. "Nothing. It's just one of those things I wanted to talk to you about."

"Why?"

Nadia moved her glass away as if she wanted nothing to get in the way of her message. "What did you get for helping Holly? Huh?"

"What is that supposed to mean?"

"It means how many times has she called to thank you, or Eddie or his dumb sister? How many times has Grady asked you to join them for softball? Or Kristin and Monica Miller? How many times have they called you up and asked you to come and hang out with them?"

JT looked down at the green tablecloth. How could any of them call to thank her, when none of them knew that she was the one to thank? She didn't want them to know. Still, Nadia's message was hitting home. JT was all alone now, and Nadia knew it.

"I thought so," Nadia triumphed. "It's just like Denis Daniels. You tried to help him, and in return he almost got you killed."

JT's whole body contracted. It was as if Nadia had tapped the pain center that led to JT's every nerve. Denis. Beautiful, sad Denis. JT loved him, but he never really cared for her. All she'd succeeded in doing was making his life so bad that he'd taken her for a hopeless drag race up in the hills. She still had nightmares of the crash and the blaze, both of them being pulled out just in time to see the car explode in a burst of flames.

"How did you finally find out that I was with Denis when he crashed?" JT managed.

"Mrs. Daniels told my father. It was dumb to think I wouldn't eventually hear about it."

"Oh." JT wanted to get up and leave. Even being all alone was better than this. Nadia knew her every sore spot, and that's just where she threw her punches. JT had little energy left to resist. She felt as though she might just crumble onto the floor.

"Have you heard from Denis? Did he call to say he was sorry for almost getting you killed?"

Nadia was plunging further into the core of JT's hurt. No, Denis had not called her to say anything. She had heard he was going away to Hawaii to join a program for troubled kids. JT waited every day for him to call and say something: good-bye, I forgive you, I'm sorry, I'll think of you ... anything. "Denis is leaving town soon. I'm sure he'll call before he goes."

Nadia's brown eyes were hard and pointed, like two dowels of dark wood. "Denis isn't going," she said with a cruel smile. "He's *gone*."

JT's breath stopped. She felt as if she were suffocating; those fires were sucking up all her air and turning her heart to lifeless dust.

Nadia kept right on going. "He left yesterday. His mom told my father. And nobody knows when he's coming back."

JT knew the color had left her face. She just couldn't believe that Denis had really left without saying good-bye after everything that had happened. No note. Nothing. That's how much JT meant to him. Nothing. Wood scraped against linoleum as JT backed up her chair. She was about to leave, when she felt Nadia's hand on hers.

"JT, wait."

Nadia's voice was much kinder. The kindness made JT stay, but she heard a tinge of the old Nadia neediness that kept her on guard.

"I know this is all painful to you, but I'm just doing it to prove a point. Did I warn you to stay away from Denis, or didn't I?"

JT looked up. Lines of tension creased Nadia's tanned forehead.

"I just don't want to see you hurt again. I'm not sure you know who your friends are anymore. That's why I want to give you another chance."

JT felt a little dizzy. She was still thinking about Denis, his ghostly face as they watched his car go up in flames. Now he was gone.

"Everybody will be back soon. Lisa flies in from Europe in a few days, and Mindy gets home tomorrow. Even Glennie will be back from London in a few weeks. I'm willing to start over if you just say you're sorry."

Mindy and Lisa. Superrich Glennie Taryton. JT pictured the other girls from the social crowd and felt even more lost. She had never really fit in with them. It was just that she was so glad to have popular friends that she didn't care what they were like.

JT reached for a couple of bills and placed them on the table. She felt so alone. But she took strength from remembering what she had put up with as Nadia's best friend. Even feeling empty and scared was better than that. "How can I say I'm sorry when I'm not?" she whispered. "I meant what I said."

JT intended to get up and leave, but Nadia's enraged face riveted her. The gorgeous brown

37

eyes were full of outrage, and the veins in Nadia's neck were showing. JT didn't move.

"Do you mean that?" Nadia seethed.

"Yes. I do."

Nadia's eyes started to unfocus as though she were making JT disappear from the face of the earth. JT had seen Nadia do this to plenty of others—people she felt were so insignificant they weren't even worth looking at—but JT was shocked how little she felt now that Nadia was doing it to her. She was already nothing—how could Nadia make her feel she was any less?

"Fine," Nadia spat out. "Then you'd better be ready to hear some things that *I* mean."

JT looked around, suddenly conscious of the rising volume of Nadia's voice. She was glad the restaurant was almost empty.

Nadia stood up and leaned over the table. "JT," Nadia announced, "you are a zero. You were a zero when I found you, and every friend you had was because of me. Without me, you will be a zero again." Nadia looked her up and down. "So go back to being fat, unpopular Janet Terry Gantner. You won't need my help with that. You're already on your way." The sandal spun and Nadia was gone.

Quivering, JT stared in front of her. What she had always feared had just happened. Nadia was probably right. She might very well turn into the hopeless fat girl she was before. Leaning her head back, JT put her hands to her baby-soft cheeks and felt the beginning of tears.

It was okay, she told herself over and over. Cry alone in a restaurant, eat yourself silly at home, mope around the cookie store—anything was better than crawling back to Nadia.

That was the one thing she had learned from the whole mess with Denis. What had happened was worse than anything she ever could have imagined, and somehow she had survived it. Even finding out that he had left without saying good-bye—that was what she feared most of all.

JT pressed a paper napkin to her face and sat up. She didn't know how she was going to start over. It was possible that by the time school started again, she would be as fat and reclusive as she'd been in junior high. But even so, she couldn't just give up. No. She hadn't gone through all of this just to let people walk on her for the rest of her life. Janet Terry Gantner was at least going to give it a try.

4

"QUIET IN THE STUDIO, PLEASE. LET'S TAKE IT
FROM THE TOP OF THE SCENE, FELICIA'S LINE,
'WHAT ABOUT THE BABY?'"

The voice filled the cavernous television studio
coming from somewhere behind the cameras and
the microphones and the countless crew members in Levi's and tool belts. Amy was stretching
her neck, hopping from side to side, anything to
catch a glimpse of the action. She still couldn't
believe she was really here, and she didn't want
to miss any of it. But her view was blocked by a
low rack of lights and a huge camera that rolled
as smoothly as an electric floor polisher. She
froze, almost shushing herself when she heard
the actors begin the scene.

"What about the baby?" moaned Felicia, a hand on her stomach.

"We can go away somewhere," answered a clipped male voice.

Amy recognized the British accent at once. Nothing could stop her from positioning herself where she could get a look at the heartthrob of the Ontario High junior class, Cole Stewart. Almost crashing into an aproned hairdresser, Amy crouched down, finding a space through which she could spot the set. Cole was facing the actress who played Felicia, holding her with restless passion. Amy steadied herself with a hand on the cement floor. Whenever she saw any guy as handsome as blond, clean-cut Cole, she got that wacko out-of-control feeling.

"HOLD IT," the voice came back over the loudspeaker. "RELAX FOR A SECOND. THERE'S A PROBLEM WITH THE MIKE."

The two actors relaxed, but for Amy the adrenaline was still kicking. She knew she should be thinking about an angle for her story, but she kept getting sidetracked. First it was the way all the actresses were in curlers and bathrobes, looking about as glamorous as kids at a slumber party. Somehow that had shattered Amy's preconceptions right off. Then the shock that Munson Flats, the town where *Reflections* took place, was just that—a series of two-dimensional flats and doors that led nowhere. Every time an actor made an exit, Amy would watch to see where he went, only to find that the law office led to the Munsons' living room, which was just the other side of the police station.

But the most distracting thing of all was the close proximity to Cole Stewart. Amy had never seen a TV star in the flesh before. In person he was every bit as gorgeous as he was on the screen. Amy wasn't sure why that surprised her, but it did. Just looking at his strong jaw, serious eyes, and full sexy mouth made Amy feel as if someone was blowing lightly on the back of her neck. It was strange, because other than his good looks, Cole was totally different from the guys Amy was usually attracted to. There was nothing weird or eccentric about him, no earring or long ponytail. Of course, there was the exotic accent, the fact that he was a soap opera star ...

Stop! Amy smiled at herself. Roll your mind back to where you were before—find an angle for the article! Shaking her head, Amy thought how dumb it was to let her imagination go on about some TV actor just because she was in the same room with him. She had about as much chance of even talking to Cole Stewart as she did of having an article published in *Seventeen*. Down to earth, Amy. She looked back up at the set and Cole stepped into her view.

Shading his eyes from the bright lights, the actor looked up. He was about eighteen or nineteen and wore pressed white slacks and a cable knit tennis sweater—a stark contrast to the other actors, who were lounging around in old jeans, scratching their stubbly chins.

"May I change the next line to 'All that matters is that we're together'?" Cole asked the invisible voice. "Just saying 'It'll be all right' doesn't seem strong enough for my character."

The voice—actually the director hidden away in the control booth, answered, "GOOD IDEA, COLE. OKAY, FOLKS. WE'RE READY UP HERE. TAKE IT FROM THE SAME PLACE."

The camera smoothed along the floor again, and this time a wardrobe lady picked the spot just in front of Amy to park herself while pinning up an older actress's hem. Frustrated, Amy took out her pad and made a few notes. She'd been there since six-thirty. So far she'd seen part of the first blocking rehearsal, which was held in a cold basement and consisted of the actors stumbling around, scripts in hand, deciding when and where to move. Now was the camera rehearsal in the studio. After lunch would be the dress run-through and final taping.

As Amy started to write, she felt a soft hand on her shoulder. Monica stood above her in baggy lavender overalls, her face devoid of makeup and her dark hair hidden under a towel.

Amy smiled up at her.

"I have something to tell you," Monica whispered. Anxious not to disturb anyone, Monica gestured for Amy to follow her out of the studio.

Nodding, Amy tiptoed past the prop room and

the stacks of electrical cable, finally through the heavy door and into the hall. On this side of the studio door, actors chatted freely. Rock 'n' roll could be heard above the hammering and scraping in the scenery shop.

"How's it going?" Monica asked.

"Great."

Monica smiled. Since Amy'd met her at the movies the previous night, she'd been amazed how unsnobbish and friendly the actress was.

"I found one cast member who was willing to do an interview over the lunch break. You'll kind of be on your own. I have to set my hair."

"Thanks. Who do I get to talk to?"

Monica took off her towel and rubbed her wet head. "I tried to think who kids in St. Cloud would be interested in, and I figured they'd like the girl who plays Felicia, 'cause she's our age and all. But Laurel—that's Felicia—she's kind of a snot and she wouldn't do it, because you weren't from some big magazine. But I found somebody else, so it's okay."

Amy was sort of relieved she didn't have to interview Laurel. The stunning actress looked fifty times more intimidating than Sandy Bennett, the girl whose father owned the biggest mills around St. Cloud. Thinking up questions to ask a girl like that would not have been easy. "Who did you find instead?"

Monica casually fluffed her hair and started

back toward her dressing room. At last she turned around and gave an innocent smile. "Cole Stewart."

For the second time in two days, Amy Parker was speechless.

"Don't worry. I don't know him very well, but he seems like a really nice guy," Monica assured her, one hairpin in her mouth, both arms over her head.

Amy swallowed hard. She was sure that was true, but it didn't help keep her knees still. They were knocking together, actually knocking. Amy was glad she wasn't skinny, or the clunking bones may have echoed off the dressing room walls. She had really done it this time. After years of dares and plunges, jumping first and looking later, Amy Parker might finally be in over her head.

Monica pinned up the last curl and plopped onto the carpet, her script between her legs. It was so quiet now. The door was open, but the corridor was like a hospital. When someone walked by, they did it soundlessly.

Lunchtime seemed to be time to study lines, shower, shave, generally get ready for the afternoon of shooting ahead. Monica had pulled a sandwich out of her backpack. With the other hand she covered part of her script, only to peek back at the lines, like someone testing herself for a final exam. Amy stalled in the doorway and watched her. Finally Monica looked up again and seemed surprised that Amy was still standing there.

"Cole's dressing room is just down the hall on the other side. His name is on the door."

Amy smiled and almost giggled. Great. Just what she needed to do when she interviewed Cole Stewart, giggle like a moron. "Okay. See you later." She hoped she sounded professional. Forget professional. She hoped she sounded sane.

Totally absorbed in her work, Monica raised two fingers and waved. Amy pulled the door shut.

The corridor was plain beige, and Cole's dressing room wasn't more than twenty feet away. But Amy couldn't help thinking that those were the longest twenty feet she'd ever travel for the *Ontario High Express*. One foot in front of the other, Parker. You've known how to do this for a long time. Come on. One foot in front of the other.

Rap rap rap. She had arrived.

No response.

Amy knocked hard. Whack whack.

"No need to pound the door down," came those crisp British tones from inside.

Embarrassment heated Amy's cheeks. She grimaced, and her wheat-colored hair fell across her face.

The knob turned from inside, and there he was, standing in front of her in a white terry cloth bathrobe, his blond hair wet and slicked back. His cheeks were pink from the shower, and he smelled of aftershave—some grassy, floral smell that reminded her of the woods back home. Amy tried not to breathe too deeply; the aroma made her feel lightheaded.

"I'm sorry I knocked so loud," Amy blurted. She was amazed that any words came out at all. "I thought you didn't hear me."

"It's all right." Cole stepped back and offered a hand to shake. At the same time he did something like a little bow. Amy had never seen a teenage boy do that.

She stepped in, pulling the door closed behind her. His dressing room was the same layout as Monica's but much neater. Classical music was playing on a small tape recorder, and there was a vase of flowers in the corner.

Cole leaned up against the counter and gestured Amy to the chair in front of him.

"Welcome." He smiled. His teeth were white as unblemished paper. "I'm Cole."

A tray with a sandwich and a cup of fruit salad sat next to him on the counter. Next to that was a white porcelain teapot.

"I'm Amy Parker." Amy's voice felt as if it were coming from a ventriloquist, it seemed so disconnected from her body.

Cole was relaxed. He picked up half his sandwich. "Excuse me for eating, but it's the only time." He paused to take a few bites. Amy noticed a square of smooth chest peeking out under the collar of his robe. She looked away. "And I did want to talk to you."

"You did?"

He laughed and poured some tea. His laugh was easy, more like a chuckle. "Tea?"

Amy shook her head. She was in no state to be trusted with dangerous objects like breakable cups and hot liquid. He poured his own, savored the aroma, and sipped. There was something about him that was so unlike the boys Amy had gone to school with. Maybe it was just how polite he was, how gentlemanly. Whatever. Amy was fascinated. She opened her pad and set it on her lap.

"It's really nice that you could talk to me. Thank you," she said, picking up his good manners. Amy often found herself adopting the qualities of people around her. It was a trait that sometimes got her in trouble, but in this situation she figured picking up Cole's elegant dignity would only do her good.

"And why shouldn't I talk to you?"

"Um, well, because I'm not from a real paper; I mean, it's just a high school paper."

Cole watched her, amused. "So? Don't real people read your paper?"

"Yes."

"Then it's a real paper."

He smiled again, and Amy started to relax. "I guess it is."

He put the rest of his sandwich aside and wiped his hands. Just sipping his tea now, he concentrated on Amy with the full force of his rich brown eyes. Amy thought his eyes were the same color as the bay pony she'd had when she was little.

"Now, Amy Parker, what would you like to ask me?"

Amy hesitated. She wanted him to go on talking. She loved the sound of his voice. "Oh. I guess I should start with how old you are."

He gave her a funny frown. "Almost nineteen."

"How long have you lived here, I mean in the U.S.?"

"Three years." He was starting to look a little bored all of a sudden.

"Do you still go to school?"

"I graduated high school here a year ago." Turning away, he put his cup down. Amy had the strange feeling she'd said something to offend him. "Amy, you know none of this matters—how old I am or if I go to school. What matters about people is how they feel, how they see the world. Don't you agree?"

For a moment Amy was shocked. Cole was looking in her eyes again, almost as if he was giving her a dare. She sat up and smiled. If he wanted to throw a curve, go off on some wild tangent, Cole Stewart had picked the right person. "Then tell me something about how you feel," she encouraged. It seemed like a good time to let the old Amy impulsiveness fly. She leaned forward. "And make it something you've never told any reporter before."

The corners of his full mouth turned up. He

was looking at her with new interest. "All right." Resting back against the counter, he folded his arms. "I feel like I was born in the wrong century."

A chill went up Amy's spine. She felt that way whenever her imagination took her somewhere really special. It was amazing, his telling that to someone he didn't even know. "You do?"

He stared at her. "Why do you have that sound in your voice?"

Amy put a hand to her lacy shirt as if she could touch her vocal chords. "I just feel that way, too, sometimes. Like I go in those old rooms they have set up in museums, and I feel like I belong there."

"Yes! And do you know why you feel that way?"

Breathless, Amy shook her head.

"Because those rooms still have poetry, romance. Look at this." He stood up and gestured to the formica counter, square mirror, gray metal locker. "How can anything happen here but the most ordinary things?" He slapped the beige counter. "It's all so bland. After five minutes, you don't even notice it's here. It's the same way with people."

Amy was riveted. She had never met anyone like him before. "What do you mean?"

"Like dating. People just hang out together till they're so used to each other it's nothing more special than this chair."

Amy lifted slightly to look at the seat of her chair. It was orange plastic, the molded kind they stack up in huge piles. She gazed up at Cole. "Do you know every chair I've seen in this studio is exactly like this one?"

He knelt down before her, his expressive hands only inches from her knees. "That's right. In the old days things were done with care and attention. No two chairs would be the same." He looked down. "And when a boy was interested in a girl, he wouldn't spend meaningless time with her until they were so tired of each other they were like those orange chairs. No, it would be mysterious and beautiful. . . ."

Amy found herself melting onto the carpet, too. Before she knew it, her denimed knees hit the bristly shag and she was staring into his face. The thrilling tone in his voice did something to her, and there was no holding back. "Yes. It would be like Romeo and Juliet. They would know there was only one person for them, and they would know that as soon as they saw the other person. They'd just feel it. . . ."

"COLE!"

Amy's heart jerked when they were interrupted by the voice outside. She suddenly felt incredibly foolish. She was supposed to be doing an interview! However had she ended up kneeling on the floor rambling on about Romeo and Juliet!

The door swung open before Cole had a chance to give permission. Amy scrambled to her feet. Cole stood gracefully.

"Cole, sweetheart," said a gum-chewing older

lady. She wore an apron with needles, clips, safety pins, practically a whole sewing kit stuck on it. "Whenever you can, come see me. Okay? We have to alter that suit for the party scene."

"I will, Lenora. Thank you."

Lenora smiled at Amy and left.

After she was gone there was an awkward silence.

"I have to finish getting ready, I'm afraid," Cole apologized. "I need some time to think about that big scene with Felicia."

Amy cleared her throat. "Of course." She had that creepy, crawly feeling that told her she had just made a fool of herself ... again. "Thanks for taking this much time to talk to me."

"My pleasure." Those brown eyes lingered on hers and the lips drooped a little, giving him this sleepy, sexy look that zapped currents down Amy's legs. She continued to the door, telling herself not to misinterpret his politeness.

"I hope I gave you enough to write about."

"Oh, you did."

"I don't believe in giving ordinary interviews."

Amy nodded. There was nothing about Cole Stewart that was ordinary. "I'll send you a copy when it's done. Thank you."

He held the door open, and his arm brushed against her shoulder. "Thank *you*. Good-bye."

" 'Bye. I'm sure I'll see you again," Amy said. Then she caught herself. She meant she would see him on the TV, but for a second she was afraid he might have taken it the wrong way. Of course she didn't mean she would be bumping into him on the street or meeting him at the pizza parlor. Embarrassed, she giggled a little and started to pull the door shut.

Cole's warm hand landed on top of hers. Amy almost gasped. His touch vibrated all the way up her arm. "Yes, you will see me." He looked at her with those sleepy eyes again, and everything inside Amy went haywire. She felt as if all her circuits had been overloaded and there should be steam coming out of her ears.

Luckily Cole pulled the door shut, because Amy was barely able to move. As she forced herself to travel the short distance back to Monica's dressing room, she went over and over his parting words.

"Yes, you will see me," she repeated dreamily. Of course, he'd meant she would be seeing him on television. That had to be it. But then why did he have that heavy-lidded gaze, that soft smile?

Amy straightened up and tugged on her suspenders. She was getting carried away again—reading things in that just weren't there.

Oh, well, she decided, even if Cole didn't mean anything by his parting remark, even if he was sitting in his dressing room right now chuckling to himself about the dumb reporter from St. Cloud—even then, it was just fine. Amy still had the experience, the memory, and the sensation. And she loved all three.

❀ 5

THE AIR WAS HUMID AND DENSE. NO ASH HERE, JUST THE collective sweat of fifty bodies grunting and groaning their way to perfection. Weights clanged, Bruce Springsteen sang over the speakers, dozens of feet thump thumped on the jogging track overhead. JT stood in the doorway to the gym, gazing at this shrine to physical fitness. It made her feel tired.

"Beverly Hills Fitness Center," announced a cheerful voice. JT turned around and saw a lithe blonde in a Superman leotard answering the front-desk phone. The girl's figure was almost as superhuman as her suit. Behind her was a poster of some amazingly muscular girl in a leather-fringed bikini—the poster said the model had "flex appeal."

JT looked down at her pale soft body, barely

hidden by a pair of gym shorts and her Hard Rock Café T-shirt. The shirt pulled across her full bust, and JT tugged at it as she sat. "Flex appeal," she muttered. "I have about as much flex appeal as a Hostess Twinkie."

Shifting, JT wiped the beads of sweat from her forehead. She had made herself come down to this gym, and now she had to stick it out! She knew that getting fat again was the first thing she had to avoid if she was going to make it on her own. Already she was well on her plump way—as Nadia had so sweetly pointed out. If she gained any more weight, she would barely have the nerve to leave her room, let alone make new friends. JT wedged her hands under her damp thighs and frowned.

Today she was starting her new program. No more samples from her parents' cookie stores. No more chocolate, ever! She had even ridden her bicycle down to join the Beverly Hills Fitness Center. But she'd almost been sideswiped on the way by a Volvo station wagon, and it was about ninety-five degrees outside. So here she was; supposedly eager to shape up and join, and she felt so nervous and defeated it was taking every bit of willpower not to walk right back out the door.

Another leggy beauty had slipped behind the front desk. She was the total opposite of JT—tall and lean, with broad shoulders and a glossy dark ponytail. JT stared at her back with envy.

The dark-haired girl was clearly an instructor, and JT could hear her lecturing a new member.

"See, you don't have to worry about getting huge muscles, because girls don't have the same hormones as guys," she was instructing.

They were interrupted by another fitness center employee, this one male. He had very short dark hair and a sunburned nose. JT immediately recognized him as fellow Sunset High senior-to-be David Michaels.

David brushed by the dark-haired instructor and commented, "Elena, don't lead that poor girl on. You have more hormones than any guy I know."

JT put her head down. She had known something was familiar about the dark-haired girl, and as Elena Santiago turned to glare at David, JT recognized her high cheekbones and spirited stance. Elena was also in her class at Sunset—although they were in such different crowds they barely spoke to each other. Still, Elena was Eddie Santiago's sister, and he was Holly Harris's boyfriend. The whole thing was too close for comfort. JT had heard something about Elena working at a health club, but she had no idea this was the one. Forget joining here. JT sat tight, waiting for a moment when she could slip out without attracting any attention.

Elena and David were facing each other. "I know it's hard for you when a mere girl can outlast you in aerobics class, but you'll get over it," she taunted him.

He grinned and put his hands on his trim waist. "A mere girl. You're a mere girl like King Kong's a mere monkey."

Elena cocked her hip and leaned over the counter, chin on her fist. She looked up at David with her big dark eyes. "Well, even a mere monkey could have lasted till the end of my aerobics class."

"Okay, Miss Hormones. I'll race you in the swimming pool any time your delicate little heart desires."

Elena threw her head back. "I never go in the water. Too much of it does something to the brain."

JT could hardly believe it. David was the star of the Sunset Swim Team and known for his stinging sense of humor. Most girls were so intimidated by him they didn't even flirt. But there was Elena, not only encouraging his barbs but handing them right back. If Elena could do that to David Michaels, what would she do to timid JT Gantner if she ever found out what JT had done to her brother's girlfriend? Beginning to panic, JT grabbed her bicycle bag and made for the door.

"JT? Is that JT Gantner?"

Elena's clear, strong voice. JT froze. She was caught. A million reasons why she had to get going right away flew through JT's mind, but not one made its way to her mouth. JT slowly turned around.

Elena was striding toward her in a red sleeveless leotard and green tights. The sight of her did not instill JT with the Christmas spirit. Briefly looking past Elena, JT noticed that David had gone back into the gym.

"Hi," JT said softly.

"Hi," Elena returned in a friendly voice. Her skin was smooth as light creamy toffee. "I didn't know you belonged here."

JT looked nervously at the racing stripes that covered the concrete walls. "I don't."

"Oh. Are you meeting somebody?"

"No. I just came to look. I already saw everything. It's a nice gym."

Elena didn't seem to pick up on her discomfort. "Who showed you around?"

A drop of sweat was rolling down the small of JT's back. "I just looked by myself." She started for the door.

Smiling, Elena stopped her. "You should at least see it right. Come on, I'll explain everything to you. That's part of my job."

Clutching her bag to her chest, JT reluctantly followed Elena back into the gym. Again there was the metal clanging and the groaning and the straining red faces. Some people were strapping themselves into machines that looked like ancient torture devices.

"There's a lot of different equipment here. Plus

aerobics classes," Elena explained. "If you join, I'd set up a personalized routine for you and teach you how to do all the exercises."

JT was barely listening. She was peering past the barbells and the exercycles into the endless mirrors that lined the gym walls. JT looked down. Lately she hated looking in mirrors.

Full of vigor, Elena was chatting on about the various features the health club offered. "What is it you mainly want to work on?"

JT raised her head. "What?"

Elena was full of interest. "Well, I mean, do you want to work on getting stronger or training to go out for a sport at school or toning up, stuff like that?"

Suddenly the noise, the mirrors, the humidity all got to JT and made her feel incredibly vulnerable. What *did* she want? She wanted the confidence to go out on her own and be liked for herself, not used by girls like Nadia or rejected by guys like Denis Daniels. But she could never say that to Elena. "I'm so fat" was all that came out.

Elena's smile faded. "What did you say?"

"Fat," JT mumbled as if it were the worst curse in the world. "I'm much too fat."

Elena looked confused. "JT"—she sounded really surprised—"you're not fat."

JT slung her bag over her shoulder and hugged her middle. She felt flesh. Too much flesh. Fat JT! "I won't be when I lose a bunch of weight," she said finally. "That's why I want to join a gym."

Elena took JT's arm and pulled her into the corner set aside for the aerobics classes. Now it was empty. Just a lifeless record player, some ballet barres, and more mirrors. JT still wouldn't look.

"JT?" Elena's voice was full of concern.

"What?"

"Do you really think you're fat?"

JT hesitated. "Of course I am."

"Look at yourself in the mirror," Elena ordered. "Come on."

JT allowed herself to see only her round baby face, so pink from the heat and the stress.

Standing next to her, Elena looked at JT's reflection and folded her slim arms across her chest. "JT, everybody's built differently. Like I'm just naturally kind of all arms and legs."

JT gave a hopeless laugh. All arms and legs was a modest way of saying long-limbed and gorgeous.

"Eddie's the same way. You're different—softer, more feminine. Believe me, there are lots of girls who wish they had more in places where you have it."

JT glanced at herself but quickly looked away.

"It probably would be good if you lost five pounds or so, but if you start exercising, that'll happen right away. You shouldn't be hung up about being really fat, though, 'cause you're just not. If you think like that, you'll end up anorexic or something."

Finally JT gathered the nerve to really look at herself. She took a step forward. For a moment she saw a curvy seventeen-year-old who was certainly not skinny but was by no means obese. Then someone else stepped into the reflection. It was the thirteen-year-old JT staring back at her—the old JT, who really had been fat, whose clothes had pulled over her belly and hips, whose legs had looked like sausages. JT took another step in, and the pretty seventeen-year-old came back. She stood there, her insides whirring as the two reflections fought it out.

"JT? What do you think?"

JT kept staring. Why did she see that fat thirteen-year-old so often when she looked in the mirror? That unhappy girl hadn't existed since JT'd dieted her away years ago. So why was JT so unable to accept the presentable, even attractive person that she'd become?

Nadia. Beautiful Nadia. JT closed her eyes and seethed. Of course. How many times had Nadia reminded her that she was just a fat girl, a chubby nothing? It was just like the way Nadia took her shopping and steered her toward the dull, blobby clothes—always dropping hints about how they would hide her problem. What problem? When JT really looked at herself, she saw she didn't have a problem! Unless not being built like a ballet dancer was a problem.

"JT, are you okay?"

Blinking, JT noticed Elena again and felt the

beginning of a smile. "I'm fine," she said. "Just fine."

Elena's face was full of questions. "Do you want me to explain anything else?"

JT turned to look back at the gym floor. This time the grunting didn't seem so grotesque, and the weight machines looked almost friendly. She saw all different types of people, plump, skinny, some attractive, some not, all working hard to make themselves stronger. That was just what she needed. To be stronger, to get used to looking in those mirrors and not having that miserable eighth grader look back. Just as they had to water and plant to reforest those burnt-out hills, it would take care and effort to rebuild JT Gantner. With a big breath she faced Elena. "You don't have to show me anything else."

Elena looked a little disappointed. "Oh. Okay. Well, if you have any questions or you decide you want to join, just let me know."

JT smiled. "I have decided."

"You have?"

"Yup." With a glance back in the mirror, JT gave a definite nod. "Sign me up."

Half an hour later, Elena sat alone in the small office, finishing the forms for JT's membership. It had been a very good day. She'd signed up three new members, taught one of her better aerobics classes, and gotten one up on David Michaels. She stretched her long legs under the desk and smiled. David thought he was such hot stuff just because he was good-looking and an All-City swimmer. He thought no girl could possibly compete with him. Ooh, she hated that, guys who thought girls were delicate little flowers that had to be condescended to. Well, he'd have to get a little tougher before he'd be able to show up Elena Santiago.

With a giggle Elena went back to checking JT's application. Janet Terry Gantner. Now, she was a strange one. Yet of all the girls in that hideous social crowd, JT was the only one Elena'd ever thought was halfway nice. Eddie'd been in a class with her and always said she was okay. And ever since Holly'd been hired at Mrs. Gantner's Cookies, Elena'd had a warm feeling for JT. Not that JT had had anything to do with Holly's job, but the association made Elena feel more sympathetic.

Elena was chewing on the cap of her pen and double-checking the figures when she heard a knock on the office door.

"Come on in."

"Hi, Lainie." It was Bev Sokol, another instructor, who'd just graduated from Hollywood High. "You busy?"

"Just finishing this membership stuff. What's up?"

Bev gave her a funny look and closed the door. After running a nervous hand through her short hair, Bev sat down next to the desk. Then she picked up a paper clip and played with it. " 'Member after I quit Camp Beverly Hills to work here and you told me if I ever knew anything about who spread those lies about Holly Harris I should tell you?"

"Sure." Bev had still been a salesgirl at the Beverly Hills boutique when two girls had come in and ruined Holly's chances for a job by saying she was a shoplifter. Thinking about the pain her brother's girlfriend had been through still made Elena burn. "Why?"

Bev snapped the paper clip in two. "Because for the first time since that mess happened, I saw one of those girls."

Elena sat up. "Where?"

"Here. Just now in the gym."

Elena was already on her feet, ready to go after the guilty party. "Point her out to me."

"She's gone. But I'm sure you'll know who she is. She was the one you just signed up. The girl with the short blond hair and the Hard Rock T-shirt."

Elena sat back down. She was shocked. "JT Gantner?"

Bev shrugged. "If that's the girl who just joined."

"Are you sure? One long earring, kind of shy?"

"The girl who was just in here. I'm positive. But she wasn't the one who did the talking. She was just along. It was the other girl that really did the damage."

"And you still have no idea who that was?"

Bev shook her head and went to the door.

Elena looked back at JT's application. Her mind was going a hundred miles a minute. "Thanks, Bev. I really appreciate it."

"Sure. See you later."

The door closed, and Elena put her head in her hands. JT Gantner! Why would JT have tried to ruin Holly? Now Nadia, or one of those other posh girls, maybe. But from what Elena had found out, Nadia had been in France at the time the whole mess happened and the others had all been away on vacation, too. It didn't make sense.

Unconsciously Elena had rolled up JT's application and was shaking it in the air. When the paper fell open, Elena's eyes focused on the date of JT's first personalized visit, the appointment when Elena would introduce her to the wonderful world of physical fitness. Hmm. That just might be a perfect time to finally find out exactly who was the cause of Holly's misfortune. And when Elena did discover who was responsible, watch out. Because Elena Santiago had every intention of making that person pay.

❀ 6

"KRISTIN," AMY WHISPERED, GENTLY TUGGING AT HER friend's sweatshirt. "Nap time is over. Time to tear up the town."

Kristin pulled the quilt up over her head and moaned. They'd been out every night since Amy's arrival, and she was beginning to feel as if her life were on nonstop full speed ahead. She couldn't remember being this tired since Amy'd taken her on a camping trip two years ago.

Amy sat on the edge of her bed and playfully pulled back the covers. "I have a present that will make you feel better. But you have to open your eyes and sit up first."

Kristin smelled something sweet and nutty. She sat up with her hands over her eyes and let Amy hand her a fresh peanut butter cookie.

"Your mom and I just made them," Amy said brightly.

"You're so industrious," Kristin mumbled. But when she put the warm cookie in her mouth, she had to admit it cheered her. Slowly her eyes opened.

"I would have let you sleep longer, but Grady'll be here to take us to that disco really soon."

"Mmmm." Kristin finished the cookie and rubbed her eyes. Her mind was starting to clear—this was the night she and Grady were taking Amy to The Pink Whale.

So far Amy had had more adventures than Kristin had experienced her first two months in L.A. First there was that incredible encounter with Cole Stewart at the soap studio, then they'd all gone to see Eddie do his stand-up act at the Comedy Club and were also entertained by a hypnotist who took one volunteer from the audience—who, of course, was Amy. Since then Amy'd interviewed a champion break dancer at Venice Beach, gotten Michael J. Fox's autograph on Beverly Boulevard, hit a bloop single to win the Sunday softball game, and witnessed a small airplane crash landing in the cookware department of the May Company. The Renaissance Fair, Monica's beach party, and who-knows-what-else were still to come, and Amy showed no signs of slowing down.

Forcing her eyes open, Kristin got a good look at her friend and had to smile. Amy was wearing her old riding jodphurs, a plaid blouse with a white lacy collar, suspenders, and cowboy boots. Her blond wavy hair framed her face like stalks of wheat. Back in St. Cloud, Amy had been known as the most creative dresser around. Here she didn't seem nearly as wild, but she still stood out with her individuality and flair.

"I wish I didn't have to go to work tomorrow." Kristin yawned. "I feel like sleeping about twenty hours straight."

Amy gave her a teasing grin and bumped her shoulder. "I don't think work is exactly the problem, sleepyhead."

Kristin picked up on the tone in Amy's voice and laughed. "What does that mean?"

"It just means I heard how late you crawled into bed last night. You thought I was asleep, but I was awake thinking about my soap opera article."

Swinging her legs over the side of the bed, Kristin tossed her long hair out of her face and shrugged. Amy was right. Every night after Amy'd go in, she and Grady would stay in the jeep for at least another hour, talking, kissing, sometimes just holding each other and looking at the summer sky. Now that there was only another month left before Grady left for Yale, they wanted to take advantage of every second.

Amy laced her arm through Kristin's and leaned her head against her shoulder. "It'll be hard when he goes east, won't it?"

Kristin looked over and nodded. Intuitive Amy,

as emotional as she was, was so aware of other people's feelings. It was part of what made her such a good friend. "Yup. He and I don't want to talk about it. We sort of pretend it's not happening, but I know we both think about it all the time."

Amy patted her arm. "You have to talk about it. Otherwise it'll get weird."

Kristin broke in. "I know. If there's one thing I know, it's how bad it is to keep stuff inside. It's so strange to think about things like should we date other people, stuff like that. But I guess it's time."

"It's definitely time."

Kristin slapped Amy on the knee and stood up, pausing to stretch her arms up to the ceiling. "What about you? Did you decide to be up-front and call Cole Stewart?" Kristin gave a devilish laugh. Amy had told her every detail of her interview with the actor, and Kristin had been kidding Amy to call Cole for a date. It was one of the few topics that could actually make Amy blush.

"Right." Amy laughed. "Maybe I should just write him a fan letter. Dear Cole, remember me? Amy who?"

"I don't know," Kristin teased her. "I think he liked you."

"Kristin"—Amy buried her face in her hands—"I'm sure I'll never see him again." She grinned. "But I still can't wait to tell everybody back in St. Cloud about what happened."

"If you want to exaggerate a little, add a few juicy details. I won't tell on you."

"Thanks a lot."

"Ah, what are friends for?" Kristin laughed. "Okay. I guess it's also time I got dressed so we can let you loose on this poor town again."

Amy nodded. "Good idea."

Kristin headed for her closet. "Why don't you run down and tell my folks where we're going. I think Holly and Elena are going to the Comedy Club to watch Eddie again, but just in case they call, I want them to know where we are."

"Anything to get you awake and moving. I'll wait for you downstairs. If you don't show up in ten minutes, I'm coming back up here and pouring ice water on your sheets."

"What did I do to deserve you as a best friend?"

"Just lucky, I guess."

Kristin smiled. "I guess so."

Pink. Everything Amy saw was pink. Pink ceiling, rose-colored floor, pink ribs along the walls to look like the inside of a pink whale. The tables were pink; the waiters wore pink jackets. The Cokes even had pink paper umbrellas sticking out of them. The only time things weren't pink was when the lights would jiggle across the dance floor, turning things lavender, then blue, then back to . . . pink.

"Sorry we can't stay really late. Legs and I have to work tomorrow," Grady yelled. They were sitting at a small table alongside the disco floor of The Pink Whale. The music was so loud it seemed as if the whole room was throbbing.

"Okay," Amy answered. They'd been there an hour already, but Amy had not tired of the hectic movement and noise. "This place is amazing."

It was amazing. Bodies gyrated and pulsed. A few guys had their shirts off; girls' shoulders and thighs wore nothing more than pale pink light. Behind the dance floor was the area called The Belly of the Whale, where videos flashed on a huge screen. Above that was the DJ's booth and powerful pink spotlights that swept over the floor picking up a couple here, a single dancer there.

The pounding beat ended, and a slow song came on. The dance floor divided—those who wanted to boogie and sweat wandered off, while the more involved couples clasped hands around necks and arms around waists and began to sway. Grady and Kristin looked at each other. The intimacy of their glance made Amy feel that she was invading something private, and she had to look away. Grady led Kristin onto the dance floor.

Watching them dance, seeing Kristin's sleepy head pressed along Grady's shoulder, his face nuzzling her hair, made Amy suddenly feel left-out and lonely. No matter how many wild adventures or brief flirtations she had, they were like junk food—they might stimulate her taste buds or keep her going for a while, but eventually they left her hungry for more. She could see from the look on Kristin's face that her friend had no desire for anything else.

Amy sighed and spun the pink umbrella that had come in her Coke. Looking up, she spotted a waiter who was smiling at her in a very unwaiter-like way—not as if he were trying to pick her up or anything but as if he knew her and he was coming over to her table to chat. Amy looked at him hard, trying to figure out if he could be someone she knew from Minnesota. Then she checked their glasses and decided the waiter was coming over only to persuade her to order more sodas.

When he arrived, she looked up apologetically. "I don't think we need any more to drink yet."

He smiled that familiar smile again. There was something smug and expectant about his stance. He reached in the pocket of his pink jacket and pulled out an envelope.

"You're Amy Parker, right?"

"Yes."

He placed the envelope on the table. For some reason Amy was surprised that the paper was not pink, too. It was white.

"For you."

"Me?" Amy's face scrunched up with confusion. She had no idea what was going on. Then the waiter took his hand from behind his back, and a long-stemmed red rose appeared. He placed the rose in front of Amy, gave another goofy smile, and left.

Amy stared at the table. She felt as if she were in some kind of dream, and all she could figure was that this was some sort of stunt to add to The Pink Whale's atmosphere. Okay. Amy was as game as the next girl. With an unsure little laugh, she opened the letter and read by the light of the pink candle.

"You are the most beautiful girl here," the note said. "I have been across the room watching you. If you want to see who I am, look into the spotlight at the end of this song. XXX"

Amy brought the paper to her mouth. For a moment she was stunned. She didn't know how to react. Was it somebody just being corny, or was it for real? If it was for real, who possibly could have sent it? She was just breathing in the rose's perfume when the song ended. Amy followed the spotlight.

She saw him immediately. But it couldn't possibly be real. It was her imagination getting so carried away that she was actually seeing things. Rising from her seat, Amy stared into the halo of the long pink glow.

There he stood, gazing at her. His blond hair glistened. He wore an old-fashioned white tuxedo jacket and baggy slacks. As he slowly walked closer, the light seemed to stick to him, and everything else faded into nothingness. But Amy still couldn't believe her eyes. It was Cole Stewart.

Slowly she walked toward the edge of the dance floor. Her heart was pounding harder than the pulsing of the lights. Her hands were shaking, her breath short—she felt as if something soft were lightly floating over every inch of her skin. A saxophone moaned low and sultry. Another slow song. When a husky voice began to sing, Amy saw Cole's hand reaching out to her.

For a moment Amy thought she should find Kristin and Grady, get some indication that this was really happening, something to remind her what reality was. But there was no turning back when she looked into Cole's eyes. His hand touched hers, and he was pulling her in to dance with him. She went.

His jacket was like felt against her chin, and the same aftershave she had smelled in his dressing room enveloped her. When his cheek brushed against hers, she had to close her eyes, try to keep the sensation in, so she didn't melt onto the floor. His hand smoothed small circles along the small of her back, and she felt the motion through her whole body, circling, spinning, till she was almost faint.

The throaty singer crooned on. Amy was afraid to open her eyes again and look. Maybe it wasn't really Cole. Maybe it was some stranger holding her. The patchy light was deceptive. Finally she opened her lids a crack and saw Kristin. Her friend and Grady were no longer dancing. They were standing at the edge of the floor, eyes wide, mouths open, staring at her. As Amy let herself look further, she saw another girl who'd stopped dancing to gawk. Finally the music faded out and the arms holding Amy relaxed. She took a step back to look in her partner's face. He smiled at her with that perfect white smile.

"Cole," Amy breathed.

It was really, truly he.

His hands remained on her shoulders, and the corners of his eyes crinkled up as he smiled again. "Surprise."

Amy was speechless. Almost.

"Do you come here a lot?" she managed. Her voice was sticking somewhere in her throat, but luckily the music was softer now.

Cole took her hand. "Never. I don't like places like this."

Amy had never met a guy who kept her so constantly off-balance. Not that she didn't like that feeling, but at this moment, she longed for something logical to hang on to. "Why are you here?"

"Looking for you."

Looking for her!! Amy's pulse was racing. "But how did you find me?"

He chuckled. "I wanted to find you. You're not that hard to find."

"But how did you know where ..."

"I asked Monica where you were staying."

"So you called and Kristin's mom told you ..."

Cole gently covered Amy's mouth with the tips of his fingers. "Don't try to figure everything out. You'll spoil it."

Amy let her forehead fall against him. She felt soft, soft cotton over a slim hard chest. He was right. Let the mystery take over. She slowly led him over to the table where Kristin and Grady stood waiting. They both had their jackets on and looked at Amy and Cole with astonishment.

"There are my friends," Amy said, making introductions.

Even Kristin giggled a little when she shook Cole's hand.

But before they could chat, the music erupted again with a deafening downbeat. Cole put his hands to his ears.

"It looks like you're about to leave," he projected to Kristin and Grady.

"We both have to be at our jobs pretty early," Grady replied. He gave Amy a protective it's-time-to-go look.

"So do I." Cole smiled. "Do you mind if I drive Amy? I promise to drop her right home."

Kristin looked first at Grady, then at Amy. She had that sensible Kristin look, the one that said, "Amy Parker, you'd better stick with me, or you'll be in over your head again." Amy ignored it.

"I'll go with Cole," Amy said before Kristin had a chance to disagree.

Kristin gave her one more hard look. "I'll see you at home"—she checked her watch—"by eleven. I'll be waiting downstairs."

Amy almost laughed. Kristin was acting just

like her mother. A lot of Amy's friends acted that way with her.

"Shall we?" asked Cole, offering his arm.

Amy laced her elbow with his. She turned back to Kristin. "I'll be home before you and Grady get out of the jeep."

Kristin broke into a loose smile and patted Amy's arm. "Okay. 'Bye."

" 'Bye."

Cole and Amy walked past the rows of whale teeth, the tongue that was really a coatroom, and the narrowing whale mouth, until at last they emerged into the cool, breezy night. The wind blew Amy's hair across her face, and she stopped under the bright lights at the disco entrance. There was a full moon, and for the first time Amy saw almost as many stars as back in Minnesota.

"Cole?"

He stopped and looked at her.

"Did you really go through all this just to find me?"

He put a finger to his lips. "Shhh. No talking."

"No talking?"

"Not tonight. Tonight is special."

He held out his hand, and Amy let him lead her out of the light, into the parking lot. As soon as they slid into his new Peugeot, he opened the sun roof and popped a tape into the deck. Something like mandolins or harpsichords filled the roomy front seat. Without a word, Cole pulled the car out of the driveway and drove up toward the nearby Hollywood Hills.

They climbed patiently until at last they arrived at a curve near the very top. Cole pulled off the road, turned up the music, and got out. He opened Amy's door, and she got out, too.

The view made her gasp. Lights in crisscross patterns went on for miles, stopping only at what had to be the ocean. Nearby hills were speckled with starry bursts, and a golden glow tinged everything.

"It's so beautiful." Amy heaved a sigh.

"Yes."

Facing her, Cole put his hands on her shoulders. She could just see the outline of his features in the moonlight—his eyes had that sleepy look again; his full mouth was slightly parted. The soothing music still floated out of the car. Everything inside surged, like crashing waves. He was going to kiss her. Amy let her head fall back and closed her eyes. Soft lips met hers. One hand was in her hair, the other supporting her back as her whole body arched, like an old-fashioned swoon. He tasted of peppermint.

Cole kissed her only once.

"I promised to get you home."

Amy found herself wishing that he was not quite so polite and gentlemanly. He opened her door, and she floated back into the car.

As silent as before, he pulled back onto the

mountain road. In minutes they were in Hollywood again, on their way to Beverly Hills.

The traffic on Sunset Boulevard moved much
too quickly, and soon they were turning onto
Rexford Drive, heading for Kristin's house. Amy
gave Cole directions, all the time not wanting to
leave the delicate music, the new car's fresh leather
smell. Cole pulled up in front of Kristin's house
and turned off the engine. The music stopped,
too.

"Will I see you again, or do I have to wait till
you magically appear?" Amy couldn't resist asking.

He rested his elbow on the back of the seat and
shifted toward her. "Hopefully there will always
be some magic about it. How about Wednesday? I
don't have to work. We could spend the day
together." His crisp British tones contrasted with
the lazy humming of the crickets.

"Yes."

He touched her cheek ever so lightly. "Just you
and me. We'll go on a picnic. Have you seen the
botanical gardens?"

"No." Amy's head swirled with visions of colorful flowers, stone benches, blankets on patches of
lush grass ... and Cole. But she remembered
something. "I'm supposed to go to the Renaissance Fair with Kristin and her friends on Wednesday." Amy frowned. As strong as her romantic
impulses were, her loyalty to her friends was just
as powerful. Still, she didn't want to miss one
minute with Cole. "But why don't you come, too?"

Cole looked skeptical. "I don't want to be with a lot of people." His full mouth had a hint of pout.

Amy snuggled close. "It's just Kristin and Grady and a few others. They're wonderful people. And the fair is all knights and ladies and wandering minstrels. You know how I told you I liked those old rooms in the museums. The fair sounds like that."

Cole was starting to look interested. "Really? Maybe it would be a good idea."

"Please. I think it sounds perfect. Will you come?"

Cole's face was soft and his eyes hazy again. He leaned in, put his hand to the side of her hair, and kissed her cheek. "Yes," he whispered.

By the time Amy had caught her breath, Cole was standing outside, opening her car door. He helped her out, and she felt like some kind of princess as he walked her to the door. But he hesitated before reaching the brightly lit porch and stayed on the dark path.

"Good night," he called.

Amy stood with her back to the door and waved. Unable to move, she watched him walk down the path and get into his car. Before pulling away, he blew her a kiss.

As the car disappeared down the street, Amy slid down along the door until her bottom collided with the cool brick. Holding her face in her hands, she began to laugh.

"This is too unreal," she heaved, the adrenaline

starting to rush through her body. She was no longer feeling romantic and delicate. She now wanted to run up and down the street, hollering at the top of her voice.

"Kristin!" she yelled. "I'm home!!"

Giggling, she managed to stand up and open the door just as Kristin grabbed it from the inside. Amy hugged her and laughed joyously, almost knocking her friend over. Amy'd had a lot of adventures in her life, but none of them had been quite like this one.

❀ 7

"COME ON. ONE MORE. THAT'S IT. DON'T GIVE UP. KEEP breathing and pull it down one more time."

JT's face was the color of an overripe strawberry. Sweat dribbled down her temples, collected on the top of her lip, and soaked the back of her T-shirt. Elena watched carefully as JT pulled the bar behind her neck and the muscles in JT's arms and shoulders began to tremble. Good. JT would be a little sore tomorrow—nothing wrong with that—and in the meantime, Elena would soon have her in such a state of exhaustion that JT would tell her anything.

"Okay," Elena chirped, marking down JT's exercise routine on a rectangular card. All around them weights were banging. At the other end of the gym, David was teaching a calisthenics class.

"Hurry to the next one. You want to keep your heart rate up so you get an aerobic workout, too."

JT nodded blearily and hoisted herself off the exercise machine. When she looked at the next contraption, she almost started to cry. She'd had no idea there were so many ways to torture a person disguised in the friendly name of exercise.

"Hop on." Elena smiled, demonstrating the position.

JT's entire body was shaking. Elena had insisted on training her on the Nautilus machines, the very ones that reminded JT of medieval horror devices. You had to strap yourself in, and once in position, JT had no idea which part of her body to move which way. When she finally discovered the point of the exercise, she wished she hadn't. She found herself wishing plump, dimpled bodies would come back in style.

Elena fastened JT's seat belt and instructed her to lift the bar above her head. "This is for your shoulders."

JT lifted the weight twice, then shook her head. She bravely put her hands up, tried to budge the weight again, but nothing happened. Elena was impressed. This was a hard exercise, and considering that JT was not in shape at all, she was making a valiant effort. Still, valiant or not, Elena went ahead with her plan.

"Eddie, my brother, said to say hi to you," Elena began while JT caught her breath.

JT looked up. She grabbed the bar and raised it again. She wasn't sure where the strength had come from, but anything was better than talking about Eddie.

Elena reached up and helped JT control the weight on the way down. "You know Holly, his girlfriend? Did you know that she's working in one of your parents' stores? The one on Doheny Drive. She's met your mom. She says she's really nice."

JT unstrapped herself and bolted off the padded seat. Why was Elena bringing up Holly and the cookie store? Another of JT's worst fears was coming true. She blindly staggered to the next machine. A sweaty man was just getting off it, and JT climbed in, imitating his position. She sat straight up, a bar against her nose, and pushed two padded cylinders back with her elbows. She felt as if she were rowing a boat.

"You don't have to do this one," Elena counseled. She was beginning to get concerned. She had just meant to wear JT's defenses down, but JT was attacking her new program with amazing fervor. As JT continued to row, Elena decided to plunge ahead. "Anyway, Holly really likes her job, and it's a good thing, because she was supposed to work at Camp Beverly Hills—she was hired and everything. But then the day before she was supposed to start, they changed their minds. And do you know why?"

JT was now pushing like a maniac. Her eyes

had a possessed glaze to them, and she was panting heavily. Elena slipped behind her and lightened the weight.

"The reason why Holly wasn't hired was that two girls went all over Beverly Hills spreading lies and ruining her reputation. What do you think about that?"

CLANK.

JT couldn't row anymore. Her arms collapsed, and behind her the iron weight crashed down on the stack beneath it. Despite the scraping and clanging around her, JT was sure that her weight had rung louder than anyone else's. She was surprised that the whole gym wasn't staring at her. She started to get up, but Elena stood in front of her, leaning on the padded cylinders. JT felt as if she were in jail.

Elena's dark eyes had turned hard and serious. "All right, JT"—she leaned in, her voice just as cutting as her gaze—"I'm going to stop being cute. One of the instructors here was working at Camp Beverly Hills when you and your friend went in. I know it was you, because she told me. I want to know who was with you and why you did it."

JT could not look at Elena. She stared at the turquoise plastic seat and watched three droplets of sweat fall on one corner. Or maybe it was three tears. Or maybe it was a mixture of both.

JT didn't know what to do. She admired Elena: her strength, her loyalty to her brother and Holly, even the bold way she was going after the truth. But JT was so confused. Her body was too weary for her to think clearly, and she didn't want to be a tattletale. Plus there was her own guilt. She made a move to get up, but Elena blocked her path.

"Tell me who the other girl was," Elena insisted.

JT's forehead fell against the metal bar. If she confessed her own role, then maybe it would be better. She would finally be made to pay for the horrible thing she'd done, and it would be over. "It was all my fault," she whispered.

Elena crouched onto the carpet next to her. Her face wasn't as accusing as JT expected. "Why do you say that? Bev said the other girl was the one who did all the talking."

JT shook her head. The strain on her muscles was catching up with her, and her limbs were vibrating uncontrollably. "I could have stopped it. I told myself it was okay—that Holly really had shoplifted—but deep down I knew it had to be a lie and it was wrong. But I just stood there and let it happen." Now there was no sweat hitting the plastic seat. Only tears.

"Why, JT? Why? What did Holly do to ever hurt anybody?"

"It was so stupid. Nadia was just mad because she thought Holly had lied to her ... you know, that awful mess when everybody thought Holly was really rich."

Elena bounded to her feet. "Nadia? So it *was* Nadia!"

JT clapped a hand over her mouth. She hadn't meant to rat on someone else.

"I thought Nadia was in Europe when it happened."

It was all out now. "The day after," JT heaved. "Nadia went to Europe the day after she got Holly fired."

Elena backed up and helped JT out of the machine. "Thanks for telling me. I know it must be hard, since you're Nadia's best friend."

For the first time that afternoon, JT smiled. But it wasn't a happy smile. It was just that everything in her life suddenly looked totally absurd. JT wiped the sweat and the tears from her overheated face. "I'm not Nadia's friend anymore. I guess the thing with Holly was what did it. It made me sick." She looked away, embarrassed. "Anyway, I'm sort of on my own now."

Elena looked at her differently. There was a touch of respect and kindness in her face.

"What other exercises do I have to do?"

Elena was still thinking about the guts it must have taken for JT to break away from Nadia Lawrence. "I think that's more than enough for your first time," she answered softly.

"Okay." Sad and almost numb with exhaustion, JT started walking back to the dressing room.

Elena ran after her. "JT?"

"Huh?"

JT looked so defeated Elena wanted to shake her. You should be proud of having thrown off Nadia, Elena wanted to yell. Proud! Suddenly a connection was made in Elena's brain, and she looked at JT with a little awe. "Did you get Holly that job at your parents' store?"

JT didn't answer.

"You did, didn't you?" Of course. How else had Holly gotten hired? She had never applied for the job. The cookie store had called her out of the blue. Elena felt incredibly stupid for not figuring it out before. She touched JT's arm. "Thank you."

JT just shrugged. "It's no big deal. It was the best I could do." She headed again for the stairs leading down to the dressing/pool area. Elena stuck with her.

"I worked you kind of hard," Elena apologized. "You should go soak in the Jacuzzi. You might be sore tomorrow."

"Oh." JT continued down the stairs.

Elena accompanied her all the way into the dressing room. JT looked so alone, so defenseless, and after all the brave things she'd done. If there was one quality Elena admired most, it was courage. She sat down on the bench next to JT's locker.

"JT?"

JT glanced over briefly before spinning the lock and opening the metal door.

Elena clasped her hands and leaned on her

elbows. "You know what you said about being on your own?"

JT didn't respond. She was staring blankly into her locker.

"Well, I was thinking. You know Eddie and Grady from when you guys were in media class together, and they both like you a lot. Josh, too. Anyway, Monica Miller is having this party Saturday night at her uncle's beach house in Malibu, and we're all going—Kristin, and Holly, a bunch of other kids from Sunset. Would you like to come? Monica said I could invite more people. You could even bring a date if you wanted." She waited for a reaction from JT. "So would you like to come? I'm sure everybody would be glad to see you."

Finally some life came into JT's slack features. She turned to Elena, her innocent eyes full of surprise. "You mean it? You would really want me to come to a party with Holly and your friends?"

"Absolutely." Elena smiled and stood up. "Will you come?"

JT's heart fluttered with wonder. "Okay."

Bubbles fizzed under JT's body. Steam rose all around, making her feel as if she were in the middle of a huge pot of soup. The chlorine was strong, and the Jacuzzi bath temperature had to be way over a hundred, but JT wanted to lie there forever. Her arms and legs were so tired it felt as though the water were gurgling them away until there would be nothing left of her but a disembodied head.

And what a confused head it was. On the one hand she felt great about being invited to Monica's party. She hadn't even dreamed of an offer so generous. She'd always liked that crowd. One Sunday she'd seen them playing softball at Rancho Park, and she'd longed to join their happy camaraderie. Of course, being Nadia's pal had always canceled out getting to know any of them. And then there was the mess with Holly. JT could hardly believe she was being given a second chance.

She sank lower in the tub and exhaled along the top of the water. On the other hand, would those kids ever accept her? And what about Nadia? What would Nadia do when she found out that JT had ratted on her?

That was JT's main regret—ratting. She hated telling on other people, and this was the second time she'd done it recently. The first time—when she'd given that reporter information on the trouble Denis Daniels had been in—that had led to Denis's freaking out and crashing his car and leaving town. And never even bothering to say good-bye.

But this was different. JT sensed somehow that it was. What Nadia did to Holly was so wrong, so cruel, that keeping it quiet would have been a sin. JT hoped that was true. She closed her eyes and let the hot water bubble over the back of her neck and the ends of her hair.

"Hello there."

A confident male voice jolted JT out of her contemplation. She had thought she was alone. At least she had been alone the last time she'd looked around the damp, cavelike Jacuzzi room. But now there was a boy sitting on the edge of the tub, looking down at her. All she noticed was his blond hair and trim smooth chest.

"Hi," she whispered. For a split second his profile reminded her of Denis—something about the way the golden hair fell over one eye, the line of the jaw. But when he turned to face her, she saw there was really no similarity at all. This boy was much more conventionally handsome; his face didn't have Denis's ruggedness or character. And his eyes were eager, hungry—they held none of Denis's experience or pain.

He lifted himself and dropped into the water beside her. JT inched a little farther away. He smiled easily. "You come here a lot?"

He lowered himself only waist-deep. JT got the feeling he sat up on the step because he wanted her to look at him. "I just joined."

"Yeah? Good deal. I work out here all the time. My name's Ken."

"I'm JT."

"Yeah? What's that stand for?"

"Janet Terry."

He looked around the room. JT felt like he was

looking for someone more interesting. When no one came in, he turned back to her.

"Where do you go to school?" she asked. He looked to be eighteen or so.

"I just graduated Santa Monica High. How about you?"

"I have one more year at Sunset."

There was a pause as JT came up out of the water. Her leotard clung to her full bust, and she caught him staring at her as she emerged. Embarrassed, she sank back down.

"So do you like working out?" Ken asked.

"I guess so."

He went all the way under the water, then came up, flung back his hair, and smiled. "It's good to keep in shape. Like I'm doing these modeling jobs now—I did this calendar that just came out—so I have to have a good body." He smoothed the water off his face.

JT fluttered to her feet. He certainly did have a good body, muscular and broad-shouldered. There was a mirror on the opposite wall, and JT caught him admiring himself in it.

"Is that what you want to be, a model?"

"I'm not really sure. Right now it beats cleaning swimming pools, which I have to do sometimes— you know, when the modeling is slow."

"Oh."

He looked up with interest when someone else walked in. But it was an overweight older woman. After glancing around restlessly, he pulled himself up and grabbed a towel. "Nice talking to you, JT," he said, rubbing the towel over his stomach.

"You, too."

He knelt by the edge of the tub and gave her a cocky smile. "I'll leave my number at the front desk for you. If you get bored some night, give me a call."

JT didn't know how to respond to that. She'd never called a boy in her life, and she couldn't imagine a guy being so confident that he'd say something like that so easily. She was glad the hot water had already turned her cheeks red, so he couldn't tell that she was blushing.

When she didn't answer, he waved and strode off, pausing briefly to admire himself again.

After he left, JT pulled herself out of the water. The heat had made her a little dizzy, and her limbs felt as if they were made of rubber. Trying not to slip, she tiptoed across the tile, grabbed her towel, and went back to the dressing room.

She knew this was an important day in her life. Getting invited to Monica's party, having a great-looking guy try to pick her up. But somehow she couldn't digest it all yet. She knew this was only the beginning. There was still a very long way to go.

8

AMY SHIVERED. A SHUDDER TRAVELED FROM HER BARE ankles up to her lace-gloved hands. She looked over at Cole, blinked, and smiled. Briefly letting go of the steering wheel, he ran his hand from her cheekbone to her chin. Amy shivered once more.

"It's so nice to be with you," he whispered.

The shiver turned to a rumble and a rush.

"Let's keep reading," he said.

"Okay."

Amy reopened her copy of *Romeo and Juliet* and read out loud. Cole wanted to hear the scene again where Romeo visits Juliet's balcony. He knew all of Romeo's lines by heart, and as she read, he answered back in his passionate actor's voice.

He finished his line, and it was her turn. Even

though Amy'd read the play before in school, it was hard getting her tongue around those old-fashioned words. She was glad when it was Cole's turn again, and he launched into a long speech. Leaning back against the soft leather seat, she breathed in the poetry and the thrilling sound of his voice.

They were on the freeway, heading toward the Renaissance Fair. Already they'd been on the road an hour, and the city was gradually fading away behind them. The fair was east, almost to the desert. Trees disappeared until the rolling hills were covered with only yellow-brown bushes, patchy grass, and occasional balls of tumbleweed.

But to Amy the parched scenery seemed like a movie going by. Inside the air-conditioned car, it was so cool she rubbed her arms to keep warm. A soulful flute played over the tape deck, and beautiful Cole sat driving in beige pants, a cotton shirt, and wide-shouldered linen jacket. He looked as elegant and clean as a new snowfall.

"Do the speech at the beginning again," Amy urged. "The one about the moon and the sun."

Cole smiled. "You like that one?"

"Oh, yes." Amy loved the part about Juliet's eyes being so bright they could take the place of the stars.

Cole began to recite.

Amy still couldn't quite believe this whole thing was happening. Any moment she expected to open her eyes and find out it was all a dream. She'd even made Kristin and the gang wait until Cole picked her up before going off without her—she was that unsure he would really show up.

But show up he did. And with a red rose in his hand. And here she sat in his Peugeot, listening to him recite Shakespeare on her way to this magical fair. It was a good thing she was belted into her seat, because she felt like jumping up and down, laughing for no reason, generally acting like a total goof. But goofiness—falling into pigpens or giggling uncontrollably—that definitely was not Cole Stewart's style. Amy folded her hands, took a deep breath, and tried to look composed.

" 'O! that I were a glove upon that hand, That I might touch that cheek,' " Cole finished.

Amy closed the book. They had been reading the play since he picked her up at Kristin's, and it seemed kind of dumb to go through it again. But as soon as the pages touched, she felt a tinge of apprehension. She suddenly wasn't sure what to talk about—which for Amy was unusual. Everything was such a romantic whirlwind with Cole that it seemed weird to bring up things like how many brothers and sisters you had, which rock groups you liked, or what your favorite subject was in school.

So Amy looked at Cole instead. In the late-morning light, his hair was the color of fresh corn silk and his jaw seemed a perfect right angle. His brown eyes watched the road, but every so often he would glance at her, and when he did, every thought was rocketed out of her head.

He did it just then—looked at her. His hand left the gearshift and slid on top of hers. Amy was sure that every nerve in her palm had just become a thousand times more sensitive.

"We're almost there," he said.

Sure enough, there was a sign alongside the freeway instructing them to take the next exit. The lettering on it was ornate, and it was decorated with drawings of ladies in puffy gowns and men crossing swords. Amy sat forward with anticipation.

"I can't wait." She sighed.

"Me either."

Cole cast his eyes on her again, and she no longer cared that she couldn't think of anything to say. Why talk when she felt like this? Words could never describe the whirling that was going on inside her. She didn't know what *would* describe it. All she knew was that Amy Parker was madly in love.

"Eddie!! You are really asking for it. I always wanted to put a dead fish in your bed, and now I think I finally have a good enough reason."

"Aw, come on. It felt good, didn't it?" Eddie ducked behind Holly as his sister came at him. "No! Holly, protect me!"

Holly giggled and held his arms behind his back. "Forget it. You're on your own."

"Oh, no! It's the feminist women's ice collective. Grady, they're ganging up on us. EEEEHHH!" SHHHOOOOOOSH.

A jumbo-sized paper cup full of melted ice had just been dumped on Eddie's head. The water beaded up on his curly brown hair and ran down his face, leaving dark streams down the back of his bowling shirt.

"Hey, that feels good. Do it again." Eddie laughed.

As soon as his sister, whose hair was also dripping, raised the cup again, Eddie grabbed it and went for Kristin. He just missed her head but managed to soak her bare shoulder and the straps of her light cotton tank top. Laughing, Kristin jumped so far off the front seat she almost hit her head on the roof of the old station wagon.

"Hey, that does feel good," she said with mock seriousness. She flung a few drops at Grady.

"Uh-uh," he teased. "Leave the driver out of this. One of us has to be a responsible adult."

They all grinned at one another, then at the open ice chest. It had been filled with ice, sodas, and Fudgsicles. But in no time Eddie and Holly had eaten all the ice cream, Elena, Kristin, and Grady had polished off the soda, and now they were keeping cool by pouring the melted ice on one another's heads. The desert air was so hot the water dried almost immediately.

"Hey, responsible adult," said Eddie in a high voice. "I'm carsick."

Elena giggled. "Yeah. I have to go to the bathroom."

Even quiet Holly joined in. "I'm hungry."

Grady turned back with a fake snarl. "Ah, quiet, all of you, or I'll leave you off here and you'll have to suck on a cactus."

They all sat back, still and quiet—for about thirty seconds.

"Are we there yet?" Eddie whined in a child's voice.

Grady raised his hands in playful exasperation. "I think our load is just too heavy. We're going to have to sacrifice one member of our crew. Now, who is it going to be?"

Taking the game seriously, they all looked around.

"Well, it can't be Grady, because he was the only one who knew where to put the water when the car overheated," said Holly.

Grady flipped his sunglasses up and smiled. "Thanks, Hol. I'll remember that."

"And it can't be Holly, because she brought the food," Eddie added. He nudged his girlfriend with his elbow and whispered. "You're supposed to save me now. Lie. Anything."

Holly crossed her slim arms and gave him a sly shrug. "Without Elena we'd never have known when we needed a quart of oil."

Eddie slumped down. "They always turn on you."

"And without Kristin," piped up Elena, "there'd be no car."

Kristin grinned. The station wagon was old and didn't have air conditioning, but it was hers. "We all know who that leaves," she sang, "and it sure looks like a brutal desert out there. Poor Eddie. They found him demented, crawling toward a mirage. He was sure it was the Comedy Club." She turned all the way around to face the backseat. "Oh, wait." She pointed to a sign on the left. "We're here. Just in time. It's down to the wire, but Eddie gets to stay!"

"Phew." Eddie wiped his brow. "Next thing I know, you'd be dividing me up for dinner." Holly kissed his cheek, and he slung his arm around her. "You're such a group of cannibals."

"Oh, Eddie." Holly smiled, her delicate face full of love. "How could we go on without you? After all," she said devilishly, a new cupful of water in her hand, "you brought the ice!"

SHHHOOOOOOSHH.

They all applauded.

Dust. The Renaissance Fair seemed to be held on a huge plot of dust. Every footstep raised a brown cloud. The ballad singers were coated with dirt; the crafts for sale in the booths looked filmy. Even the fruit tarts tasted of grit. Whenever a dingily dressed knight or lady went by on a horse, the surrounding crowd broke into a chorus of coughing.

"I've never been to anything like this before. Have you?" Amy asked, hoping to sound upbeat.

Cole tried to smile as they kept walking.

Not only was it dusty; it was hot. Amy had heard the expression "It's like an oven out there," but she'd never understood what it meant until now. The air really was like the inside of a stove, and she felt like a lambchop sizzling away in the broiler. Luckily she was able to strip down to a lacy T-shirt and short culottes, but Cole was still in his jacket and slacks.

"Oh, look," Amy squealed, her voice full of desperate cheer. She had just spotted some kind of puppet show beginning across the dirt lane. She started for it, but Cole was hanging back. He was trying to maintain a brave front, but she could tell he was not having a good time.

"Amy, can we sit for a minute?"

Amy smiled weakly. "It's kind of hot, isn't it?"

Cole dropped to a wooden bench. He seemed to be willing himself not to sweat. "Kind of."

"Stay right here," Amy volunteered. "I'll get us some lemonade."

"Would you?"

"If that doesn't work, I saw a pond over there. There're already three geese, a swan, and some ducks in it. Maybe if we ask them nicely, they'll let us take a dip."

Cole attempted a laugh. A miserable chuckle came out.

Amy cleared her throat. "I'll be right back."

She took one last look at Cole's flushed face and hurried in search of a drink booth.

Amy could hardly blame Cole for being in a bad mood. The Renaissance Fair was not quite what she'd expected. Instead of delicate music and beautiful damsels, they'd so far seen part of a terrible play, shared a questionable meat pie, gotten dirt kicked in their faces by a crew of dancers, and had some girl dressed as the queen yell at them for not bowing when she passed. Despite all that, Amy still found things to like—the jugglers were great, and a fortune-teller had promised her lifelong happiness. But she understood how Cole could hate this whole thing.

Amy turned to glance back at him. Cole was sitting on that hard bench, looking as though he'd rather be anywhere but where he was. She couldn't stand seeing him so out-of-sorts. She felt so responsible. After all, it was her idea to come here. The worst part was she didn't know what to do to make things better. It was as if all her overwhelming joy had been stamped out in this field of endless dirt.

Amy was just getting into the lemonade line when she heard a familiar voice.

"Amy! We've been looking all over for you!"

It was Kristin. She was wearing Grady's sunglasses, a tank top, cutoffs, and a baseball cap. Right behind her were Eddie, Holly, Elena, and Grady. They were all as sloppily dressed as Kristin and looked—amazingly—just as happy.

Kristin ran over and put her arm around her. "I just won the bow-and-arrow contest!"

Amy smiled. "Congrats."

"Where were you? I thought we were going to meet at the scribe's booth."

Amy bought two lemonades and stepped aside. "We waited for you for about twenty minutes, but you didn't show, so ..." She didn't want to admit that Cole had gotten impatient at her friends' being late, so she'd given up waiting. Kristin brushed back a few stray hairs that had escaped from her long braid. "You must have just missed us. The car overheated, and we had to pull off twice to put more water in." She looked behind her. The others were across the square, watching a fire-eater. "Where's Cole?"

"He's sitting down by that lute player."

"Elena wants to do this ladder climb thing she does every year. It's just over there." Kristin pointed to the left of Grady. "Why don't you meet us there?"

"Okay."

Kristin rushed over to her friends, and Amy headed back to Cole. As she got closer, she saw that he was standing up, surrounded by three girls. He smiling and signing autographs. Relieved that the day wasn't a total disaster, Amy joined him.

"Sorry, girls, I have to go," Cole said as Amy approached. His voice no longer had that dull, annoyed sound. He took the lemonade and drank it thirstily.

"Fans?" asked Amy, smiling.

He shrugged and touched her hair. "You're the only fan I care about."

Amy was so glad to have the old Cole back she impulsively threw her arms around his neck and hugged him. When she let go, he held her just a moment longer. Amy loved feeling his shoulder against her cheek.

"You okay?" she asked. "I'm sorry it's so dirty and hot."

He smiled. "It's not your fault."

"I found Kristin and everybody. They're over there doing some ladder climb. Do you want to join them?"

He sipped his lemonade and smoothed back his hair. The charming Cole was back.

"Lead the way."

Amy took his hand and led him off to join the others.

It was a long ladder made of rope and rose at about a ten-degree angle. One end was attached to a tree stump, the other to a tiny low castle made of brick and cement. Suspended only a few feet above the dirt, the Elizabethan ladder climb looked easy. But Elena knew better. She'd tumbled off it plenty of times before.

"The secret is to balance your weight really evenly," she told her friends as she wiped her palms on her nylon running shorts. "Otherwise it flips over, and it's crash 'em, smash 'em time."

Amy held Cole's hand as they watched. The whole group surrounded Elena: Kristin and Grady, Eddie and Holly. Besides the six of them, there was a crowd of about twenty more gathered to see the next person take on the rope climb.

Elena was crouched over, as if she were about to take off in the hundred-yard dash. Her body looked strong and graceful, her long dark hair was pulled back in a now-haphazard ponytail, and she smiled excitedly at the thought of the physical challenge.

Shifting so that she stood in front of Cole, Amy sighed. He slipped his arms around her waist, and she noticed a few girls in the surrounding crowd whisper and point. Cole noticed it, too. He smiled. Amy patted his hand and leaned back against him. A warm wave went through her as she caught sight of girls staring at her with envy.

"All right," announced Eddie as Elena prepared to grab the ladder, "it's the human fly. Weak men shudder when she passes by. Strong men beg and weep."

Elena rolled her eyes at her brother. "Can it, Eddie. One more word and you get on this thing next."

Eddie held up his hands defensively and stepped back.

Elena's face tensed with concentration. The ladder attendant, a guy dressed like Robin Hood, waited for her nod and took a step back. With a leap she grabbed the sides of the narrow ladder and wedged her feet onto a lower rung. Immediately the ladder flipped over, so she was hanging upside down. The crowd gasped, but Elena showed no signs of losing her grip. Carefully she removed one hand and started to climb. A foot. Another foot. Both hands. The ladder was now perfectly balanced.

"Way to go, Lainie," cheered Eddie in a soft voice, anxious not to break her concentration.

"That's it," Holly whispered.

"You got it," Grady pitched in.

Elena was in control now. She continued to climb, and it suddenly looked as easy as scrambling up a jungle gym. Her angular face was relaxed, and when she reached the end and jumped off, she landed with the grace of a gymnast finishing a routine.

"Yaaaaayy!" The crowd applauded.

Elena laughed. Arms across her waist, she bowed cornily. "Thank you. Thank you."

As the crowd's attention followed Elena, Amy felt Cole's arms leave her middle. He was walking toward the ladder, and the next thing she knew, he was standing next to it holding on to one of the lower rungs. Looking back at Amy, he smiled.

"I remember doing this kind of thing when I was little," he said, his accent attracting the attention of those who didn't already know who he was.

Elena cocked her head and wiped the sweat from the back of her neck. "It's not quite the same." She smiled.

Cole had already grabbed both sides of the ladder and was putting his loafered foot on a rung. Elena stopped him.

"Have you ever done this before?"

Cole looked around at the crowd and smiled. "It doesn't look too difficult."

Elena did not let go of his arm. "Go ahead and try, but you really should take this off." She touched his pale linen jacket. "It's pretty easy to fall."

Cole faced her. "If one is going to do something," he said dashingly, "one should do it properly." Readjusting his expensive jacket, he gave Amy one more smile and grabbed the ladder again.

Elena shrugged. "Okay."

The crowd gathered around and was very quiet as Cole prepared to hop on. Bending his legs, he took off with great energy. He leaped, held onto the sides, and slipped his feet onto the rungs. But the force of his jump had caused the ladder not just to tip but to spin. The attendant tried to help Cole regain his balance, but the force of the spin was too strong. Over and around it went, totally out of control. For one second Amy caught the expression on Cole's handsome face—shock and total disbelief that this was happening to him. Next thing she knew, there was a thud, a gasp, and a huge cloud of dust.

There was a second of shock, then all six of them were hovering over Cole.

Grady was the first to offer a hand to help Cole up. Cole refused to acknowledge Grady's gesture. He was unhurt but was coated with brown dirt from his cheeks all the way down his beige jacket to the cuffs of his off-white slacks. Even his blond hair was darkened with dust. If Amy'd thought he looked annoyed before, that was nothing compared to the anger in his face now. He slowly pulled himself to his feet.

Amy rushed in and started brushing off his jacket.

"I can do it!" Cole spat out. Amy stepped back, hurt by his unkind tone. His lower lip was quivering, and there was a furious unseeing look in his eyes. Some of his fans were wandering away. With short slaps he wiped the dirt from his sleeve.

The attendant in his Robin Hood costume came up to Cole. He was about seventeen, with buck teeth and bad skin. "Not quite as easy as it looks, is it?" He laughed.

Cole's cheeks were reddening under the layer of brown.

"That girl sure did it good, though," the attendant continued.

Amy prayed the jerk would have the good sense to shut up.

But the attendant baited Cole again. "She just climbed up this thing like it was nothing."

Cole spun around and faced him. "Maybe if you

hadn't held it for her, she might have fallen down, too."

Intimidated by Cole's anger, the nerdy attendant gave a lame smile and backed away. As he did, Elena stepped in.

"He didn't hold it for me," she said in an even voice.

Cole was dumping the dirt out of his shoes. "He didn't?"

"No. It was just the same for me as it was for you. I've just done it before. I told you it was hard."

He looked at Elena as if to say she was very naive. Amy wanted to step in and end the argument right there, but she was still in a state of shock over Cole's angry outburst.

"I'm sure they didn't set this up for you quite the way they did for me," Cole confronted her. "I saw him holding it for you. I'm sure they do that whenever a girl tries it."

Now Elena thrust her shoulders back and raised her chin. Amy saw Eddie put his face in his hands, and she knew trouble was coming.

"Oh?" Elena provoked. "I see. Because I'm a girl, they had to make it easier for me. There's no way a dumb girl could just be better at something than you are."

Amy had seen hints of Elena's temper before, and she knew how quick she was to respond to anything that smacked of male chauvinism. Trying to make peace, Amy took Cole's arm. "Come on, you guys. Who cares? It's just a dumb rope ladder."

"No," Elena insisted, "there's a point to be made here." She faced Cole. "I warned you how hard this was. Just because your masculinity is threatened, don't blame it on me."

Amy was starting to feel ill. She wanted to clap her hand over Elena's mouth.

Cole just got more furious. "I wouldn't worry about my masculinity if I were you," he accused her, "especially considering the fact that you are about as feminine as a steam roller!"

Elena put her hands on her hips. "Oh, really?"

Amy was on the verge of tears. She felt as though any second Cole and Elena were going to start duking it out.

"Stop it, you two!" Kristin finally yelled. She walked up to Elena and grabbed her arm. "Lainie, drop it. It's not important."

Elena looked a little embarrassed. She glared at Cole one more time before joining her brother and Holly. "Sorry," she muttered.

Kristin touched Cole's arm. "Forget it. Let's all get something to eat," she said sweetly. "Come on." Everybody started to wander off toward the food booths.

Amy stood by Cole's side, but he was not making a move to join her friends.

"You okay?" she whispered, looking up at him.

"I'm fine."

Kristin and Grady had stopped about ten feet away to wait for them. "Let's go," Amy encouraged.

Cole had that pouty look around his mouth again. He glanced in her direction, but she wasn't sure he really saw her. "No. Let's leave. Let's go somewhere else by ourselves."

Amy was starting to feel as if she were being punched and pulled. "Cole, don't take it so seriously. Elena just likes to argue."

"That's not it," he shot back. "I just want to go somewhere else." He brushed more dirt off his pants leg. As he did, Kristin came back over.

"You guys coming?" she asked gently.

Cole looked at Amy. "Sorry," he answered with a stiff smile. "Amy and I are going somewhere by ourselves."

"But we were all going out together afterward," reasoned Kristin. "Don't be silly, Cole. Come on."

"Yeah," Amy agreed. She had never deserted one of her friends, and she was not about to start now. "Let's stay a little longer." She smiled hopefully.

But Cole was still steaming. "Amy"—he looked right in her face. His brown eyes were cool and demanding—"you have a choice to make. Either you stay here with them, or you come with me. One or the other. Which will it be?"

Amy couldn't believe he was putting her in this position. She'd known him less than a week. Kristin had been her best friend for ten years. She was far away from home. How could he ask her to desert her friend? When she looked in his handsome, angry face, she felt even more torn. How could she forsake Cole, special, romantic Cole. She'd never met anyone like him in her life, and she probably never would again. If she sided with Kristin and Elena, would things between her and Cole be over? She closed her eyes, straining to come to a decision. Her insides churned.

Finally she looked into Cole's face, her vision dimmed by the sun and the dirt. "Cole"—she put her hand on his arm—"I have to stay with Kristin. I'm out here to visit her. Please don't make such a big deal out of this. I care so much about you. Let's both of us stay."

His jaw tightened, and he stood stiff and tall. "Very well. You've made your choice. I don't know that we'll ever see each other again."

With that, he turned and headed off. All he left behind was a tiny puff of dust.

9

"YOU DIDN'T HAVE TO MAKE FUN OF COLE LIKE THAT. He'd just taken this terrible fall. Of course he was angry."

"He wasn't hurt. And I didn't start it. He was the one who said they held the rope because I was a girl."

Amy turned away from Elena and looked out the car window. The sun was setting, and as they neared home, the streets alongside the freeway started to be cluttered with stores and housing tracts. The traffic was getting thick and slow. To Amy the ride seemed endless. Whenever she thought about the way things had ended with Cole, she felt like crying out. How had she let him run off like that? How had she managed so quickly to blow the best romance she'd ever had?

Elena's back was to her. They were at opposite ends of the car seat, as if physical contact with each other would be distasteful. The others seemed to be avoiding them, too. Kristin and Grady sat up front, listening attentively to the Dodger game. In the very back Holly and Eddie were stretched out, napping in each other's arms.

Elena flung back her dark hair and looked over her shoulder. "Cole just can't handle the fact that a girl can be the center of attention instead of him. He probably wants girls to be like those dopey damsels at the fair."

"He does not."

Elena smiled. "But I'll tell you, if I were a damsel in distress, I'd feel safer rescuing myself than waiting for him."

That jab caused Kristin to tear herself away from the ball game and turn around. "Come on, Lainie. Don't be so hard on him. Cole's a nice guy."

"I never said he wasn't nice," Elena continued. "I just think he's a little out of touch with reality, that's all."

Amy shifted angrily. "What is that supposed to mean?"

"The way he left in a big huff like that. How dramatic can you get? It's a good thing he's an actor. I don't think he knows the difference between a soap opera and real life."

"That's not true!" Amy insisted. She knew she wasn't fending off Elena's accusations very well, but she couldn't think of anything else to say. She just knew how she felt—tied up and aching to see Cole again. She could only hope that he would show up at Monica's party Friday night. That might be her only chance to ever see him before she went home.

Amy faced the window, and the wind slapped her cheek. It blew her hair into her eyes and mouth. She suddenly felt as if she were boiling over. There was just too much going on inside, and some of it was going to have to come out.

She knew she had gotten carried away again, but unlike so many other times, it wasn't fun anymore. No longer was her relationship with Cole some wonderful adventure. Now it was a big hole, something that had been taken away—something she would probably never get back. With a shudder and a sigh, she put a hand over her mouth, and before she knew it, tears were wetting her cheeks. She continued to cry, silently, hollow with hurt, until she felt a gentle hand on her shoulder.

Amy was surprised to see that it was Elena.

"Amy," Elena said softly, "I didn't mean to make him so mad. I guess I didn't think."

"Well, you should have." Amy turned back to the window and didn't say another word the entire way home.

"Amy, just go to sleep. You'll feel better in the morning."

Amy shook her head. She sat across the bedroom from Kristin, perched on the folding cot and staring into nothingness. The more she thought about Cole, the more distressed she became. Clutching her knees to her chest, she didn't care if she never slept, never ate, never spoke again.

Kristin was on the floor doing situps. Amy did not know how Kristin could act so blasé when her life was completely falling apart.

"I know how you get when stuff like this happens," Kristin insisted, panting as she jerked up and down. "I've seen it before. But believe me, you're taking it much too seriously."

"I am not."

Kristin stopped exercising and raised her hands. "Okay. I won't remind you about the guy who played guitar for that band in St. Paul or the one you met last Fourth of July after the parade."

"They were different."

Kristin smiled sympathetically. "Maybe you'll see him at Monica's party."

"Maybe." That's all Amy could hope for. Even so, Monica's party was two whole days and nights away. How could she possibly wait that long? Besides, Cole might not even show up. And then what would she do? Come next week, she would be back on the plane to Minnesota. There was not a minute to waste.

Kristin walked over and patted her shoulder. "I have to go to sleep. I'm on the early shift at the restaurant tomorrow. Are you okay? Is there anything else you want to talk about?"

Before Amy could answer, there was a knock at the door.

"Amy?"

"Come on in, Mom."

Mrs. Sullivan stuck her head in the doorway. She had short blondish hair and small features. "Amy, honey, someone's on the phone for you. You can take it in the kitchen."

Amy jumped up off the cot. Her heart was pounding, but she told herself not to be too hopeful. It might just be her parents, or Elena calling to patch things up. She gave Kristin a desperate look and hurried into the hall. Cautiously, holding on to the railings for support, she lowered herself down the stairs and then ran through the living room.

She closed the sliding door to separate the kitchen from the main hall and sat down at the small corner desk. The receiver lay casually on top of a pile of mail and an L. L. Bean catalogue. Amy uttered a short prayer and lifted the phone to her ear.

"Hello?"

No response. Tell me who you are! Amy felt like screaming. Don't leave me in this agony one more moment!

"Amy?"

"Yes?"

It was him.

"Hi."

"Hi."

"I guess you got home all right."

"Yes. You too."

Another silence.

"Are you angry with me?"

Amy almost started to cry again. Angry? All she could think of was how ecstatic she was that he had not given up on her completely. "No. Are you mad at me?"

"No." He sighed.

Amy heard the shush of his breath against the phone. For some reason it made her remember the feeling of his mouth against hers. She softly touched her lower lip.

"Amy, I'm so sorry that things went wrong. I never should have left you there like that. Can you forgive me?"

Can I forgive you? Amy rejoiced. And she'd been so afraid that he would never forgive her. "Of course. I understand."

"Thank you."

For almost a minute Amy just sat there, cradling the phone to her ear. Neither of them said anything.

"Can I see you tomorrow night?" Cole asked, finally breaking the silence.

Amy's tears started again. Not that she was sad any longer; she just felt so much there was no other way to express it. "I'd like that."

"Would you let me make you dinner at my apartment?"

"Oh, yes."

"I can't wait to see you again. What we have is much too special to give up so easily."

Amy closed her eyes. "It is."

"So I'll see you tomorrow night?"

"Yes."

"Sleep well."

"You, too."

"Good night."

"Good night."

They both hesitated before hanging up. When she finally did break the connection, Amy burst into tears. She felt so incredibly happy.

✽ 10

"AM I GLAD TO BE HOME," COMPLAINED LISA WHITE. "I was never so bored in my life. Don't ever let your parents take you to Europe. If I ever have to go to another museum, I'll puke."

"I loved Hawaii," bragged Mindy Lockwood as she picked through a rack of designer dresses. "I met three gorgeous guys. And look"—she held out her bare brown leg—"you'd never get a tan like this here. This is definitely a Hawaii tan. Don't you think so, Nadia?"

"What?"

"My tan. Isn't a Hawaii tan better than an L.A. tan?"

When Nadia didn't answer, Lisa piped up. "It is, Mindy. Like, it's a huge difference, you know."

Nadia stared at her two friends. Lisa and Mindy:

one's mother was a clothing designer, the other's father a studio head. Both good-looking, rich members of the Sunset High social crowd, they were finally back from their summer vacations. Nadia had really looked forward to their return. But now that she stood with them in the middle of the Neiman Marcus department store, she felt even lonelier than before.

Mindy was holding a low-cut sweater dress up to her statuesque body. "So tell us more about what happened to Denis Daniels."

Nadia looked at the racks of new fall merchandise and shrugged. Talking about Denis made her think about JT, and every time she thought about JT, this terrible heaviness came over her. It was as if glue had been poured into her head and was drying over her brain. She blinked her eyes hard a few times, but the heaviness remained.

"I told you everything. There was an article about him in the paper, then he cracked up his Porsche, and now he's in Hawaii in some program for messed-up kids." She stopped to examine herself in the mirror. She still looked the same. Her long, reddish hair and flawless figure were no different. Why did she feel so listless? "Mindy, maybe you should have visited him while you were there."

Mindy laughed. "Give me a break."

"But what about JT?" insisted Lisa, tossing back her curly hair. "You really had to tell her off? You know, she was never really like us anyway."

Nadia bit her lip. She couldn't look at Lisa and Mindy. To save face, she'd told them that it was she who'd given the brush to JT. Well, it was sort of true. She *had* walked out on JT in the restaurant. Nadia wrapped her arms around her chest and tried to fight the depression. But there was a dull pressure behind her eyes that she could not ignore. Not that she was going to cry—she just felt as if she needed to.

"Really," agreed Mindy as she riffled through a table of sweaters. "I never would have told you this before, but I always thought JT was kind of a wimp."

Nadia started to respond when she saw something that knocked the wind out of her. The heaviness lifted, and her limbs surged with adrenaline. Walking toward her, no more than twenty feet away, was the very person they were talking about. JT Gantner.

A moment after Nadia spotted her, JT looked up. Something about JT was different, even from a week ago, when they had last seen each other. Maybe JT had lost a few pounds, but that wasn't it. Partly it was her clothes—she wore a simple sundress instead of the mannish jumpsuits that Nadia had always recommended for her. But that wasn't it, either. It was something about JT's face, something about the way she looked at Nadia.

JT held a large package. "Hi, everybody," she

said awkwardly. She tried to talk just to Mindy and Lisa. "How were your vacations?"

Mindy and Lisa glanced at Nadia sideways. "Fine," said Lisa as she turned away.

Mindy looked JT up and down. "Nice dress, JT. Did you make it yourself?" she asked snidely. JT got the message and looked down.

Nadia suddenly felt bolstered by Mindy's and Lisa's support. The three of them were in and JT was out. How dare someone on the outside tell off Nadia Lawrence! She was overwhelmed with a desire to lash out at JT, to hurt her ex-friend as JT had hurt her. Nadia placed her knuckles on her hips. "What's in the bag?"

JT looked at it. "It's just a dress. It was on sale."

Lisa giggled. "Figures."

JT flinched. Good. Nadia wanted to rub things in. It was time for JT to get some of her own medicine. "What's the big occasion? Got some hot date?"

"It's just a party," JT mumbled.

Nadia's mouth fell open. She knew JT well enough to know that her ex-friend was telling the truth. Nadia told herself to calm down. It was probably a family party, a birthday party for JT's nephew or something. "What party?"

Behind her, Lisa sighed. "Nadia, who cares. It's probably the youth club down at the Y."

Mindy laughed.

"It is not," JT burst out. "It's a party Monica Miller's giving."

Nadia felt as though she had been slapped. Monica Miller! JT was going to a party with Monica and Kristin and that whole crowd. How could JT do something like that! The betrayal was beyond Nadia's comprehension. "Who invited you?" she seethed.

JT looked around, unsure of how much to say. But Nadia wanted to know everything. She wasn't sure why, but it was vital that she discover every single detail.

JT clutched her bag more tightly. "Elena Santiago."

Nadia was appalled. Elena, Eddie's awful sister. Holly Harris would probably be there, too. What was JT thinking of? "When is it?"

"Friday night."

Nadia turned to make a comment to Mindy and Lisa, but they had wandered off to the next department. She and JT were alone. Nadia was still horrified at the thought of JT hanging out with that crowd.

"Who are you going with?"

JT finally backed away. "No one. Why is it so important for you to know all this stuff? It has nothing to do with you."

"I'm just curious." Nadia's brain was starting to work at capacity again. A plan was coming to her. She had to cover her tracks and get more info. "Just because we're not best friends anymore doesn't mean I don't still care about you. I was just thinking how all the decent guys in that crowd are taken, so if you don't want to stand around staring at the wall all night, you should take a date. That's all. Excuse me for thinking about you."

Nadia saw the confusion on JT's face and hoped she'd bought enough time to get what she needed. The idea she'd just come up with was brilliant. "So it's at Monica's house?"

JT was getting annoyed. "Her uncle's beach house. Look, Nad, it's nice to run into you, but I really have to go. See you later. Okay?"

Without waiting for an answer, JT went off and down the escalator.

Nadia watched her go, descending until the top of her blond head disappeared. Let JT go. It was all under control. Nadia had the important facts: when the party was and where. Monica's uncle's house was easy to find—it wasn't far from her father's Malibu hideaway. Nadia would have no trouble.

If JT could go to Monica Miller's party, so could she. Nadia wasn't sure exactly what she would do when she got there, but one thing was certain. Whatever she did, it was going to make JT come crawling back.

JT had that burnt-out feeling again. She rushed by the cosmetic counter, almost choking on the perfumes, and headed past the baskets and artificial flowers. Soon she was out on Wilshire Boulevard, accompanied by the exhaust and the rumbling of car engines. The heat was so thick she felt as if she had to push through it as she walked.

She should have been ready for it, the way Mindy and Lisa snubbed her. When school started again, she would see them every day—so she'd better learn how to handle it. Still, she was surprised how much their scorn wounded her. It made her feel like a leper, a total outcast, a pathetic nothing.

Rushing across the street, she spotted a coffee shop called the Ritz. Checking once behind her—of course Nadia and the others were not following—JT pulled the heavy padded door and went inside.

The air-conditioned restaurant seemed icy and dark after the noontime sun. There were U-shaped booths, waitresses in ruffled aprons, and a square glass counter with boxes of mints on it. The clientele looked to be shoppers and clerks from the surrounding banks and office buildings.

A hostess with a mop of ratted hair came toward JT. JT looked away. She didn't want to eat. She'd been sticking to her diet, and seeing Nadia had made her feel queasy. She just wanted some place to hide, away from the ashy heat, away from Nadia, Mindy, and Lisa. A sign pointed the way to the ladies' room, and JT followed it before the hostess got to her.

Once inside, JT breathed in the pungent antiseptic and stared at herself in the restroom mirror. Her moon face looked back, her big eyes full of pain and searching for answers. She had to make new friends; that was clear. Monica's party was becoming more and more important. This was her big chance. If she blew it, she might not get another.

She wet a paper towel and pressed it to her brow. Nadia's warning about the party stuck inside her like a hard rubber ball. Maybe she *would* stand around with no one to talk to, nothing to say. JT was always shy in a group, even when she knew everyone. A vision of herself sitting alone in some dim corner made her cringe and go even paler.

A little shaky, JT reached in her purse for some blush-on. As she did so, her hand brushed against a scrap of paper, and involuntarily she pulled the note out and read it.

Ken Cody—624-6052

The boy from the gym. As she'd left that day, she hadn't been able to resist stopping at the desk to see if he actually had left his number for her. He had. Maybe she should ask Ken to be her date for Monica's party. Right now she couldn't face the thought of showing up alone, and she had no idea who else she'd go with. It was always helpful to be seen with a good-looking guy. Maybe Ken would make things easier.

JT pushed open the ladies' room door and

parked herself at a bank of pay phones in the dingy hall. As she took a quarter from her purse, her heart began beating like a bass drum.

"Come on," she whispered, "you can do it. You have to."

Still she hesitated. JT had never called a guy before, and she couldn't seem to raise her hand to reach up and punch the numbers. Finally she took a deep breath and, feeling as if she were diving into a pool of freezing cold water, dropped the coin and punched the numbers as fast as she could. She didn't feel the sting until a cocky voice came on the other end.

"Yeah? Hello?"

"Um. Is this Ken?"

"Sure is. Who's this?"

JT's words tumbled out. She was afraid if she paused for a second, she'd lose her nerve. "I don't know if you remember me. My name is JT. Janet Terry. We met in the Jacuzzi at the fitness center. You left your phone number for me at the desk."

A long pause. JT felt humiliated. He didn't even remember her.

"Oh, right," he responded, remembering at last. "Hey, good deal. What's up?"

"Um, the reason I'm calling is because"—JT swallowed—"there's this beach party Friday night, and um, I wanted to know if um, you wanted to go—I mean, go with me."

Another pause. JT wiped a trickle of dampness off her upper lip. Was this what guys went through every time they asked a girl on a date? It was torture.

Ken laughed a short, low hee-hee. JT prayed he wasn't laughing at her. "Hey"—he lowered his voice—"I knew you couldn't resist calling me. This Friday night?"

"Yes."

"Sure. Why not. Sounds good. You want me to pick you up?"

"I guess."

"Okay. Give me your phone and address."

JT rattled it off.

"Good deal. See you around eight."

"Thanks."

"No problem. 'Bye."

" 'Bye."

JT hung up the phone and rested her forehead against the push buttons. She should have felt relieved, but she didn't. Her stomach was still curled up in a fist, and her hands were trembling.

This going out on your own had to get easier, she thought to herself. It just had to.

✿ 11

COLE'S APARTMENT BUILDING REMINDED AMY OF A CASTLE. It had turrets and spires and stained-glass windows. A winding staircase twisted up to his arched doorway on the second floor. In the entry was a theater poster of a woman with her hair down to her knees, braided and interwoven with flowers. Holding her breath, Amy knocked.

"Amy?"

"Yes."

"It's open."

Just the sound of Cole's voice made her insides go soft. Amy pushed open the heavy old door, and the light from inside spilled out as it opened. The living room was in white and pastels, dominated by a huge bookcase, an expensive stereo, and a sofa that looked like a giant cloud.

"Hello," Amy called, stepping gingerly inside. She had convinced Cole to let her drive over herself, so she had not set eyes on him since the fight the day before. The thirty-or-so hours since she'd last seen him seemed like a lifetime.

Cole finally rushed into the living room. When he saw Amy, he stopped. He wore a soft beige shirt, loosened tie, and pleated pants. His hair was wet, slicked back as it was the first time she'd seen him in his dressing room. As she took a slow step closer, she smelled his woodsy aftershave.

Things went fuzzy and slow for a moment as they stared at each other. It was as though they'd been separated for years.

"Did you just get home?" Amy asked, barely breathing.

Cole nodded.

"Was it okay? Work, I mean."

He held out his hands. "I had a big love scene. It was easy to play. I just thought about you."

Amy thought her heart would fly right out of her print shirt and through her striped suspenders; that's how explosively it was pounding. Cole slowly pulled her toward him, and the next thing she knew, his mouth was against hers, her hands felt the outline of his slim shoulders, and his arms were wound around her back. Together they came: short kisses, then longer ones, tiny kisses along her neck and the lobe of her ear, till Amy was nearly faint. She rested her head on his shoulder as he smoothed his hands along her back. He relaxed his embrace and looked into her eyes.

"Hello, Amy."

Amy laughed softly. "You certainly know how to make a girl feel welcome."

He chuckled, hugged her again, and led her over to the white sofa. As they sat down, the cushions billowed. Amy was suddenly aware of David Bowie on the stereo and pairs of lit candles all along the mantel over the old-fashioned fireplace. The flames seemed to flicker in time to the music.

Cole lounged with one leg under him. "I got home too late to make dinner, so we'll have to go out."

"That's okay."

"Our reservation's not until eight-thirty. I thought we could just stay here for a while."

"Sure."

They listened to the music and gazed at each other. Smiling, they gazed some more. Amy shifted. She was starting to wish the wait wasn't quite so long. She had that feeling again that she didn't know what to talk about. Maybe they would just kiss until it was time to go. Amy certainly wouldn't mind that, but she also felt that she wanted to get to know things about Cole that kissing wouldn't tell her. She tried to figure out how to start off.

But Cole broke the silence first. "I was so upset yesterday. I'm sorry I acted like that. Have you really forgiven me?"

"Oh, yes. I'm sorry Elena was such a jerk to you."

"She doesn't matter." Cole touched Amy's hair. "I've been thinking about it, and I realized I just didn't want to share you with other people. That's why I got so upset."

Amy smiled.

He looked at her more seriously. "It was so horrible to think I'd lost you that I sat up last night and made some decisions."

"You did?"

"I know you plan to leave soon."

Amy put her head down. "This Monday."

Cole stood up and walked behind the sofa. He fetched a small wrapped box from a cabinet against the wall and returned, folding down next to her again. Amy looked at the tiny package with curiosity.

"This is what I think," he said, tracing delicate circles on her hand with his finger.

"What."

"I have everything planned out. Our being together, that is. That's what I wanted to talk to you about tonight."

Amy listened carefully. She couldn't wait to hear what romantic adventures Cole had in mind for the three-and-a-half days she had left. "Well, tomorrow night is Monica's party."

Cole's pale eyebrows furrowed with confusion. "Yes. Of course we'll go to Monica's party, but that's not what I'm talking about."

Now Amy was confused. "You're not?"

He put aside the small box and clutched her hands. "Amy, I'm talking about our future. You and me. What we have is much too rare for you to go back to Minnesota and pretend that it never happened."

"I could never do that!"

"That's why we have to figure things out. Now, I thought you could move out here at the end of the summer. Maybe you could live with Kristin, or"—he paused—"with me here. That way we could be together as much as we wanted." He turned back to fetch the box again.

Amy felt as if someone had just dumped a load of wet cement on her. Not only was she speechless; she was so taken aback that she could barely move. Was Cole serious? This was a wonderful romance, one of the best adventures of her life, but did he really think she would leave her mother and father ... her friends at Ontario High ... her position on the newspaper ... to come out to L.A. by herself?

"Cole, are you serious?" She'd meant it to come out as a sweet question, but somehow her plea sounded more like "Are you crazy?"

Cole did not react to her tone. He continued to gaze at her with utter confidence. Amy wasn't sure what was going on. She had approached this experience the way she did every other adventure in her life, with feeling and abandon. But still, in the back of her mind she always knew it wasn't quite for real. He was a soap star in L.A.; she was a high school senior-to-be in St. Cloud. She wondered if she'd finally met someone who could get even more carried away than she did.

"For you," he said, reaching behind and handing the small box to her.

Now Amy saw something new in his eyes, and it scared her. Maybe it had been there all along, but this was the first time she'd noticed it. It was a kind of unseeing desperation—a need to make everything the way Cole wanted it to be rather than the way it really was.

She took the box and cautiously untied the ribbon. Cole watched her with great anticipation. When she pulled open the velvet-covered lid and saw the glistening light resting on that square of white cotton, she sank down even farther. The pillows practically swallowed her up. In the box was a diamond ring. A real one.

Amy thought her lips were moving, but no sound came out. She was in a state of complete and utter shock.

"Do you like it?" Cole asked anxiously.

"I . . . Oh . . . It's beautiful," Amy managed. That's what girls always said in the movies, and it was the only thing that came into her head.

Cole smiled and leaned his cheek on her arm. "I bought it yesterday after I got home from the fair. I wanted something to make up for what had happened." Lifting his head, he looked at her. He was so achingly handsome. "Try it on."

Amy slipped the ring on her right hand. The diamond sparkled like a thousand stars, but—somehow—she didn't like it. She longed to take it off.

Cole held her. "Amy, I love you."

She felt limp, like a rag doll, and she had to will herself to put an arm around his neck. She had the sense of being strangely distanced from him, almost as if he were a total stranger. Her heart wasn't thumping this time, and her skin did not tingle. He kissed her cheek, and she gently pulled back.

"Cole."

"Mmm." He was caressing her shoulder.

"Look at me."

He did.

"Do you really love me?"

"Yes," he responded instantly. Then his face darkened. "Don't you love me?"

That bright expectancy that Amy was usually bubbling over with had ebbed to an all-time low. She'd never before had anybody conform so fully to her fantasies, and it terrified her. "I don't know," she admitted. "I thought I did, but I guess I don't know you very well."

"You know I love you. What more do you need to know?"

Amy sat back. His accented voice was so passionate it sounded as though it could have been coming out of the television set.

"I'm not sure. I mean, we've never really talked

about things like what our families are like or where I come from or where you went to school, or ..." She saw alarm spread over his face. "I know you don't think that stuff is important, but maybe it is." She was suddenly hit with a wave of homesickness.

"No," Cole insisted. "Let yourself be swept away. How can we be swept away if all we talk about is where you live and what you like for breakfast?"

Amy couldn't believe he was telling *her* to get swept away. Wasn't that what she'd always done? Maybe she was finally learning what it was like to be the one to pull in the reins. "But we have to talk about what we like for breakfast. You say you want me to come here and live with you. Well, what if I do and I make liver every morning and liver makes you sick. Don't you think we'd have to talk about that!"

The pout was starting to return to Cole's mouth. "Amy, you are being ridiculous. I'm sure Romeo and Juliet never sat around discussing whether or not they liked liver for breakfast."

"Cole, I don't want to be like Romeo and Juliet. They ended up dead!"

Cole stood up and walked to the other side of the room. There was a tightness in his jaw, and he held his arms stiffly against his body. Seeing him angry made Amy feel more confused than ever. This had been a wonderful summer romance, the most perfect one she could imagine. But he was taking it way beyond the point where even the adventurous Amy felt safe. It was almost as if she were a helium balloon and someone wanted to let go of her string. She had to hold on to familiar ground, or she'd float off into never-ending space.

"Cole, I know! Let's tell each other three things about ourselves. Just three things that are important and private and have nothing to do with romance or mystery or anything like that. Three things about the real, ordinary things in our lives. Okay?"

He didn't react.

"Cole, please. You asked something of me; now I'm asking something of you. I'll go first."

He would not look at her.

"Cole, this is very important."

Finally he lifted his head. "Oh, all right," he muttered.

Amy climbed out of the sofa and sat on the edge of the wooden coffee table. She rested her elbows on her knees and thought. It took a minute or so for her to decide what was most important to tell him.

"Okay," she began. "First, my father sells farm machinery in St. Cloud. When I was growing up, we had a dairy farm, but two years ago my dad went broke and we had to move to a house in town and my dad had to borrow money from his brother to get started again, and it was really hard."

The expression on Cole's face became livelier. She got the feeling he couldn't resist being interested in what she was telling him.

"Second, I'm always practically going over the edge with stuff—school, guys, the newspaper, anything. Last summer after the Fourth of July parade, I fell for this guy who worked at the motorcycle shop and went riding with him out in this field and we crashed and I had to have twenty stitches in my leg." She lifted her denim skirt and showed him the scar, just under her knee.

"And, third, uh, I'm usually pretty happy when my dad isn't going broke or I'm not getting my leg sewn up. I have tons of friends in St. Cloud and I'm the best writer on the school paper and I got three A's, two B's, and one C—that was in Latin—last semester." She folded her hands. Cole was still listening. "There. Was that so bad?"

She saw something in his face change, like a tiny window being opened. That unseeing quality was gone from his eyes, and there was a thoughtful sadness instead. He looked different from the way she had ever seen him. He didn't look as handsome as usual, certainly not as handsome as when he was on TV, but Amy found herself liking him even more for it.

"Now you," she urged.

Cole leaned back against the windowsill. Kicking the edge of the rug with his loafer, he spoke so softly Amy had to strain to hear him.

"All right." There was a touch of belligerence in

his voice. "I grew up in a town called Manchester. It's a big industrial town in England—dreary, gray. In school I didn't do especially well, and there was nothing about me at all that stood out. Then, when my parents divorced, my mum got a job as a secretary from her cousin, who works for MGM, so she and I came over. And right away, because of my accent and all, I was special at Hollywood High. Then I started taking drama and I was good at it and my mum brought a friend of hers from work to see me, and then I started going on auditions and got the part on the soap."

He looked up for the first time since he'd started talking about himself. "And now people write articles about me in magazines and girls ask for my autograph, and I make money and live in my own apartment." He shook his head. "So why should I want to think about anything but what I am right now, what I am on the soap? I can make up who I am now. All the rest of it is too dreary." He folded his arms. "There. I don't know if that's three things or not, but that's all I have to say."

Amy walked over to him. For the first time, she felt something for him besides blind infatuation. The concern she felt for him at that moment was not as much fun as before, not as exciting, but it echoed more deeply. She truly cared about him. "Thank you, Cole. That's already better. I guess you can be madly in love and not know anything about the other person only for so long before it's a farce." She took his hand. "Tell me more. Tell me more about England, about when you were little."

That was the wrong thing to ask. Cole drew away his hand, and Amy saw that opening in his face slam shut. He went over to the mantel, his back to her.

"That dreary person is gone." He turned. "If that's who you want to know, go over there and talk to any ordinary boy on the bus or the underground. Not me." The anger was back in his face: the mouth was tense and pouty.

Amy felt like ice. Cole was up for wild romance, but nothing with any soul or grit in it. Just like the Renaissance Fair: reality was just too dirty. Elena had been right. Cole was out of touch. He didn't want a girl to be a real person any more than he wanted to be a real person himself.

Amy was also realizing something about herself. Despite her love of excitement and romance, there had to be some substance underneath to keep her going.

Suddenly she missed St. Cloud. Her earthy mom, slightly plump, always cracking jokes and telling Amy to calm down. Her moody dad, trying not to show how worried or how scared he felt sometimes. Her sister, Liz ... Huey, her crazy dog ... and Mr. Chapman, the journalism teacher who'd helped her grow from a scared freshman to the pro whom new kids went to for advice. Looking down at the diamond, she knew that the real Amy Parker had nothing to do with anything in Los

Angeles except Kristin. Amy tugged the ring off her finger.

"Cole, I can't accept this." She held the ring out to him.

He raised his head, his face full of passion again. "But I got it for you," he objected.

Amy put the ring in his hand, bending his fingers so that they closed around it. "No. Thank you, but I can't keep it."

His eyes flashed with emotion. "Amy!"

"I'm not moving here, Cole. I'm going to St. Cloud on Monday, and that's where I'm going to stay. Meeting you was one of the most wonderful adventures of my life. And in a few days, I'll go back home and I'll remember just how wonderful it was."

"No," his voice rang out. His face had gone pale, and he let the ring drop onto the carpet. "Then you don't love me after all?" When she didn't answer, he fell onto the couch. "You might as well go right now. What's the point of spending another moment together?"

Amy was stunned. She just wanted to be honest, to touch earth a little. She hadn't expected to be banished from Cole's life. Besides, she had seen a lovely, vulnerable part of him, and she wanted to see more. "We don't have to always be madly in love, do we? Can't we just have a good time sometimes, just talk?"

He looked at her with great disappointment.

"Until we get so used to each other we are like those orange chairs in my dressing room?"

"Sometimes familiar things are nice, Cole. They're comfortable."

Cole turned his head. His emotion was as grand as when he acted on television. "I don't want comfort." He would no longer look at her. Braced against the arm of the sofa, he guarded his eyes with the flat of his hand. "Go home. Go back to Minnesota. Obviously, you are not who I thought you were."

Amy crouched on the rug in front of him, trying to get him to look into her eyes. "But how could you think I was anyone! You don't know me well enough."

"You don't understand. You just don't understand." He turned away from her and buried his face in his hands. He was crying.

She watched him for a few minutes. Usually the most sympathetic person around, Amy found something about Cole's grief untouchable. She almost felt he did not want to be comforted. He was too lost in the whirlwind of his own emotions. Torn and confused, she backed up into the doorway.

"Cole?"

He flicked his head.

"Do you really want me to go?"

He nodded.

"Can't we go out and talk some more?"

"No."

Amy looked down. She still cared about him

and couldn't bear to leave him like this. But she also felt that there was nothing she could do for him if she stayed.

"Will I see you at Monica's party tomorrow night?"

He would not answer.

"Cole! Please come to the party. Otherwise I may not see you again."

Slowly he raised his head. His face was flushed and his eyes watery. "I'll be there."

Amy would have run over and hugged him, but he turned away, making it obvious that no more was to pass between them. Feeling just like an actress in an old movie, Amy whispered good-bye and swept out the front door.

❀ 12

"WHY IS IT THAT AT EVERY PARTY THE GUYS ALWAYS SET up the stereo and the girls fix the food?"

Elena Santiago stood in the wood-and-glass living room of the beach house, waving a sour cream carton at Josh and Eddie.

"Are you kidding?" Josh fired back. He stood up to clean his aviator glasses on the sleeve of his rugby shirt. "Monica's uncle has a fit if she even touches his system. Every time she gets near it, the tone arm jumps halfway across the room."

Eddie raised a piece of wire. "Yeah. It's the stereo that's chauvinistic, not us. Besides, Holly sent me in here because she said I was messing everything up."

Elena laughed. She was in too good a mood not

to. The party was just beginning to come together. The wires to the speakers were being plugged in, Josh was cuing up a record, and she could smell something wonderful in the kitchen. The entire house buzzed with the expectation of everyone knowing they were about to have a great time. The first ring of the doorbell only added to the anticipation.

"Do you want me to get it?" Elena called when Monica did not appear from the kitchen. Holly came out instead, a barbecue apron almost to her ankles and her wavy blond hair piled atop her head.

"Monica says you should be the greeter and get the door," Holly told her. "We'll finish everything in here."

"See? They don't want you in there, either," Eddie teased.

Elena grinned and then looked through the window of the modern A-frame. Outside she saw a tiny blue sportscar. The first guests. Elena happily opened the door.

"Welcome to the Miller Malibu Manor...." Suddenly Elena's throat closed, and nothing more came out. Standing in front of her was David Michaels, her fellow employee from the fitness center.

"Hi," Elena finally managed.

"Hi," David said in a clipped voice.

They stared at each other, and neither said anything more. Finally David smiled, and Elena immediately felt defensive. He always made her feel that way with the amused look he had on his face, his dark hair so short and unruly from the constant dunking in chlorine. So what if David was a first-class swimmer—the best on Sunset's team. He was also pretty rude and egotistical, and faster to start an argument than ... Elena didn't even want to think about it. "Well, I guess we just can't stay away from each other," David laughed. "I know how much you've missed me."

Elena's cheeks went hot. She hadn't really thought he'd be there. Who had invited him? Probably her brother. Very cute, Eddie.

"I can't tell you how much."

David shifted his wide shoulders, his taut muscles visible under his dark T-shirt. "You know Randy?"

For some reason Elena hadn't noticed the girl standing next to David. It was Randy Tate, a Sunset High diver. Elena suddenly found Randy's button nose and skimpy halter top very irritating.

"Hi, Elena."

"Come on in."

Elena looked away as the two of them squeezed past. For some reason David and his dippy girlfriend had made her good mood go right out the window. She hadn't felt so annoyed since that silly argument with Cole Stewart.

"So how ya been, Elena?" David prodded, stalling beside the door. "Won any good arguments lately?"

"More than I've lost."

"That's not the way I heard it. But I just thought I'd check."

Elena smiled. "Yeah, well, if you really want, you can check right back out. Nobody'll miss you."

When she saw David's face harden, she stopped. Elena hadn't meant for her quip to come out so nasty, and she saw the angry look on David's face as he led Randy on into the living room. As two more carloads of partygoers pulled up, Elena found herself thinking how often she lost her temper only to wish a moment later that she could take it all back. And what was it about David Michaels that set her off in the first place?

It was a dumb thing to worry about, she decided. Dumb. Or was it? Puzzled, Elena opened the door.

"So I posed for that calendar, and this lady who was the photographer's assistant—she had to be at least thirty—she couldn't keep her hands off me. Man, it was outrageous. A week later she calls me to come in and interview for this other job. But it was no job she was calling me about. Whoah—no, sir."

JT tried to appreciate Ken's story as they shuffled up the sandy walk. It wasn't easy. They were just arriving at the party, and already she was tired of hearing him brag about his incredible success with women. So far he'd told her how the secretaries at the modeling agency made passes at him, how the housewives he cleaned pools for drooled over his body, how girls bought his calendar just to have his picture over their beds at night. He seemed to think that any female who laid eyes on him could not resist throwing herself at his feet.

Still, as JT neared the beach house door and took a deep salty breath, she was glad that she wasn't alone. She could hear the music and the laughing and the waves hitting the ocean side of the foundation. Her stomach unsteady, she managed to lift her hand and rap quietly on the door.

"Elena, somebody's here! Where's Elena?" she heard a male voice holler. Elena. JT hoped it would be Elena at the door. JT had this tiny fear that someone else would swing open the door and say, "JT Gantner? Who invited you?" Then the door would slam shut, and she'd have to spend another hour in the car listening to Ken's tales of conquest and feeling like a fool.

The door opened, and JT's stomach turned over. It wasn't Elena standing in front of her. It was Holly Harris. Terrified and filled with guilt, JT froze.

"Hi. I'm Ken. What's happening?" Ken said immediately. He smiled at Holly and looked past her at the noisy crowd in the living room.

"Hi," Holly responded in her breathy voice. Her

eyes were the palest blue. JT felt sicker than ever at the thought of how she had hurt her. "Come on in. There's stuff to eat and drink in the kitchen."

"Good deal," said Ken, heading in that direction. JT started to follow. A delicate hand stopped her.

"Go on, Ken," Holly told him. "I have to tell JT something. She'll be there in a second."

Ken nodded and was on his way.

JT stood in the doorway, the panic swelling inside her. Could Elena have invited her just so they could all have a chance to pay her back?

But Holly's Alice-in-Wonderland face was devoid of cruelty. If anything, she looked more open and outgoing than JT had ever seen her. "JT, I just wanted to say thank you for getting me the job at your parents' store. Elena told me everything." Now Holly looked embarrassed. "That's all."

JT was overwhelmed. "But I ... I mean it was partly my fault that ..."

Holly shook her head as if to say it didn't matter anymore. "That's in the past." She held out her arm. "Welcome to the party."

JT wanted to hug her, but she was much too shy. Instead she went into the kitchen to find Ken.

By the time Amy arrived with Kristin and Grady, the party was in full swing. So many kids were dancing in the living room the floor looked as if it were wriggling. The back deck was packed: kids were even starting to spill out onto the sand. There were jocks, student body officers, Monica's friends from acting class, Josh's buddies from summer school, neighbors, and even a few pals of Monica's uncle's. But among that whole houseful of people, Amy could not find the one who mattered most. So far Cole had not shown up.

Kristin and Grady settled on the back deck. She was sitting on his lap, and they were both laughing, heads together, at some shared private joke. Although Amy knew they'd welcome her company, she decided to go off on her own. She wanted to search the house for Cole one more time.

Amy wondered if Cole would show up at all. Would he just let her leave without a chance to end things right? She knew she couldn't stand that. She hated having things unsettled. At least when she had smashed her knee or fallen in the pigpen, there was an exciting end to her adventure. Now, even though she knew Cole was not the boy of her dreams, she craved a last act to this play the two of them had created. Amy wanted a finale. But it was already after nine o'clock and Cole was nowhere in sight.

She found herself in the kitchen amid a stack of dirty dishes, a tub of ice, and three girls gossiping and squealing with laughter. Amy saw the wall telephone. She'd tried to call Cole five times already, but he hadn't answered. Her hand was on the phone before she'd decided to try again.

Amy punched Cole's number and waited. Ring. Ring. Five times. Ten. No answer. Again. Where was he?

The girls were giggling more loudly, and something was burning in the oven. Realizing that the sliding door in front of her led to the deck outside, Amy opened it. She stepped onto the wooden deck and let the misty breeze toss her hair. Walking to the edge, she stared at the glistening beach and the dark water. Not knowing what else to do, she stepped down and wandered out onto the grainy, cool sand.

"Amy? Amy, is that you?"

Elena was sitting at the edge of the water, the waves licking her bare feet, when she saw Amy's compact frame approach the waterline and Amy look out at the horizon. Amy turned. Her jeans were rolled up, and the moonlight reflected off the clips of her suspenders.

"It's me—Elena." Elena was glad to see Amy. Ever since her encounter with David, she had been brooding about how often she lost her temper, got defensive and haughty when it just wasn't called for.

"Oh, hi." Amy's voice sounded wary. She wrapped her arms around herself and tested the water with her toe.

Elena shifted back and forth in the sand, making a perfect identation for her bottom. She pulled her knees up and shook her long, thick hair.

"Amy, I'm sorry about the other day with Cole. I didn't have to do that." She hesitated. "Anyway, I'm sorry."

Amy turned and looked at her. A sad smile crossed her face, and she slowly sat down. "Thanks." Amy made a dent in the sand with the side of her palm—like a karate chop. "It wasn't your fault. A lot of what you said was true. I just didn't realize it then."

"Well, still, it was pretty dumb of me to tell you anything about guys. I don't exactly know what I'm doing in that department myself."

Amy laughed sadly. "Who does?"

"Yeah. Anyway, I wanted to tell you I was sorry for being such a creep. You didn't deserve it."

Amy smiled. "Don't worry. I'm not mad at you. Honest."

"Okay."

Elena sat with her for a few more minutes, and they both watched the waves tumble in, the spray chilling their faces. Elena started to get the feeling that Amy really wanted to be alone. Now that she had taken a break and made her apology, Elena felt like rejoining the action. She stood up and brushed the sand from the backs of her legs.

"I'm going back in. You wanna come?"

"No, thanks. I think I'll take a walk."

Elena had known she would say that. Amy looked preoccupied. She touched Amy's shoulder lightly. "See you later. Don't stay out here too long."

"I won't."

Elena trudged back up toward the house. The music and voices got louder, the light brighter. She could even smell the lighter fluid that some-one must have been pouring on the barbecue.

Instead of going up the stairs to the back deck, Elena decided to walk around the side of the house and in the front door. She slowly padded along the wooden porch, by the master bedroom, the large living room window. Elena couldn't re-sist stopping to look in.

She knew who she was looking for, although she wasn't sure why. David and Randy. But she didn't see them. She did spot JT looking slightly uncomfortable, standing next to a handsome blond guy. Feeling guilty for not being there when JT'd arrived, Elena picked up her pace. She liked JT. She wanted to make sure that her new friend felt welcome.

But as Elena rounded the corner, she stopped dead. A red Mercedes convertible had just slowed down in front of the house, and now it was park-ing no more than half a block away. As the driver got out, Elena saw her long reddish hair and low-cut white dress. She couldn't believe that Nadia Lawrence could really be headed for the beach house. No. It had to be a mistake

But to Elena's amazement, Nadia kept coming. Backing into the shadows, Elena watched as Nadia paused to recheck her makeup and pinch her cheeks.

Who could have invited Nadia Lawrence? No

one in her crowd; that was for sure. Her aggressive instincts taking over, Elena almost bolted out right there to confront the social queen, tell her to turn around and go back where she came from.

But for once Elena reconsidered. Nadia sauntered up the walk and knocked on the door. Josh answered, and though his voice was full of questions, he let her in.

"Wait a minute," Elena whispered to herself.

Suddenly her outrage turned to great expectation. She'd thought she would have to wait until school started to get her revenge on Nadia for what she did to Holly. But when a situation presented itself, one had to take advantage of it.

"Hello, Nadia Lawrence," Elena said softly, clasping her hands together.

This might be one party they would both remember for a long time.

❈ 13

THE FOAMY WATER ROSE, JUST LAPPING UNDER KRISTIN'S arms. Gasping, she jumped back. Her teeth were chattering and her elbows knocking against her sides. But when Grady came up behind her and she felt his smooth chest against her back, the chill disappeared.

"Look out!" Grady laughed. The crest of a huge wave hung over them, blocking out the dark sky for just a moment before it came crashing down.

Together they tumbled. The water pushed this way and that. Grady's arm brushed against her, then his leg. Just when it seemed that the current would hold them down forever, it forced them back up, into the cool night air.

Kristin flung back her wet hair and twined her arms around Grady's neck. His skin was slippery, and she had never felt so much of it against her body. She slid her cheek along his shoulder as he pulled her in tighter and tighter.

"Hey, who's out there?" yelled someone from a lantern-lit porch. It was the house next to Monica's party, and Grady and Kristin ignored the cry. They were too happy alone in that endless dark water—no one directly on the beach in front of them, just the tiny stack of their two neatly folded towels.

Kristin let go of Grady as she paddled over the next wave, the straps of her leotard clinging to her shoulders. She kicked playfully when Grady's hand caught her leg. He surfaced a second later, his dark hair plastered to one side, still holding on to her ankle. They laughed.

Treading water, they came together again. Their mouths touched, and Kristin felt that they were part of the same thing, the sea, Grady's legs, her arms. Kissing wildly, they strained and gulped till they both almost went under.

Grady panted. Pressed so close to him, Kristin could feel the quick beating of his heart.

He kissed her neck and whispered, "Found floating on the Malibu shore. Two teenagers out for a night swim. Drowned when they forgot to come up for air."

Kristin giggled and swam away, knifing through the water with a catch-me-if-you-can kick of her feet. Fighting the current, she swam all the way to shore, every few feet feeling Grady's hand on her calf.

Exhausted, she dragged herself out of the surf and ran as far as she could before dropping down on the sand. Grady ran in the other direction, picked up one of the towels, but still managed to catch up to her in time to cover her shoulders with it as she crumbled. He snuggled in next to her. Now it was quiet. No motion but Grady's labored breathing and the nearby crashing of the surf.

"Legs, you cold?" Grady whispered.

"No."

"Me either."

They were both shivering like crazy.

Playfully Grady gnawed on her bare shoulder. Then he turned his head, brushing his wet cheek along her arm. At the same time they both cocked their heads and looked up at the dark, sparkly sky.

They sat like that, arms wrapped around each other, legs entwined, for a long time. The party was barely audible in the distance. As they gazed at the ocean and the perfect summer sky, they were both thinking how sad it was that summer could not go on forever.

"I made my plane reservations today," Grady said finally.

Something inside Kristin didn't want to admit she'd heard him. Grady at Yale—Grady not next to her sharing a single beach towel. She didn't want to think about it.

"Exactly three weeks. I go in exactly three weeks."

Kristin closed her eyes. She turned to Grady and slipped her hands around his firm waist. He smelled salty and clean.

"It seems like a long time away—and a really short time, too."

Grady sighed. "I know."

"What do you think will happen?" Kristin found herself asking. She had thought about it so many times. "I mean, when you go away? Do you think we'll want to go out with other people? Maybe we'll just drift apart."

They huddled close and looked into each other's faces, lit by the moonlight. "I don't know, Legs." He smiled. "But I can't imagine being as crazy about anybody as I am about you."

Kristin kissed his mouth, his soft familiar mouth. She knew what he meant. All that was certain was how they felt about each other now. The rest was just too far away. "Me, too."

Then Grady laid the towel flat and they stretched out on the sand.

"I love you, Legs."

"I love you, too."

As they fell into each other's arms, Kristin was acutely aware of every sensation, every move. In another month that memory would be all she had.

* * *

Inside the brightly lit living room, JT was surprised to find herself having a good time. Eddie and Josh were friendly. Elena had made a big point of welcoming her before rushing off for some mysterious reason. Even Ken was turning out okay. Girls looked at her with envy, and since he'd arrived at the party, he'd confined his conversation to Santa Monica High, cleaning swimming pools, and new cars.

From where they stood, she could barely see out onto the deck, the party was now so thick with people. But when JT heard that voice with that determined edge to it, a sharp pain went through her, and she hoped that it was only a horrible figment of her imagination. Then she turned around and saw that lush mane of red hair, the perfect body in a wispy cotton shift pushing through the crowd. She knew her good time had come to an end.

"JT!" called Nadia, waving her hand as if JT would be thrilled to see her.

JT looked for somewhere to run to. But she was surrounded on all sides. Even worse, Ken was staring at Nadia with more than a little interest.

Nadia shoved her way closer. She looked sensational. Her shoulders were bare and tanned, and her mouth was glossy with fresh lipstick.

"What are you doing here?" JT asked at once.

Nadia put a hand to her mouth as if she was

insulted by the question. "I was at my dad's, and I just noticed some Sunset people going in here. So I decided to stop by and say hello." She sexily flipped her hair behind her ear. "Who are you?" she asked Ken, drawing her finger along his wrist. Her voice oozed seduction.

He wagged his head a little, imitating her come-on. "I'm Ken Cody. Who are you?"

Nadia took a step forward, almost pushing JT back into the crowd. "I'm Nadia Lawrence. Where did old JT ever find a gorgeous hunk like you?"

Ken threw back his shoulders. "We met in the gym. Wanna feel my muscle?" He offered her a posed bicep. Nadia touched it, her brown eyes lingering on his. He was practically drooling.

"Ooh," Nadia cooed.

That fist was clenching again inside JT as she watched Nadia's charming little show. JT understood exactly what was going on. Nadia wasn't interested in Ken. He wasn't her type any more than the scores of other guys Nadia used and cast aside. But Ken was not the point here. JT was. Nadia was out to humiliate her, and JT knew it.

JT wasn't sure why, but it was very important that she not let Nadia win this power struggle. Maybe it was being accepted by Holly and Elena, maybe it was getting used to being on her own, but JT felt she had to fight this one out. If she sat back and let Nadia win, she would feel like a total zero again, and again.

JT took Ken's arm. "Let's go into the kitchen. They barbecued some hot dogs."

Nadia blocked her path, her shoulder colliding with Ken's chest. "We can get some out on the deck. They'll be better that way. Right off the grill."

"Yeah," agreed Ken. "Let's go out onto the deck."

Nadia led the way. Ken followed her. JT stuck close to Ken. She was not letting him out of her sight.

Once out on the deck, Nadia squealed, "Oh, it's such a great night." She ran down to the sand, Ken on her heels, before JT could stop her. "It's a perfect night to walk on the beach"—she looked up at Ken—"don't you think?"

He could not take his eyes off her. "Good deal."

They were almost down at the shoreline when JT caught up. "Ken," JT demanded, barely getting her breath, "let's go back in. I'd really like something to eat."

"Oh, JT," Nadia said, giggling, "it's all that eating that got you in trouble in the first place."

JT wanted to slug her. She was suddenly angrier than she had ever been in her life. She had to stand up for herself.

"Ken, I'd like to go back!"

He barely glanced at her. His eyes were fixed on Nadia. "Relax. It's nice out here. We can go back pretty soon."

"Yeah," agreed Nadia. "Relax, JT. Maybe we

should take a walk. I know of some great caves near here."

Ken was more than ready. "You do?"

That did it. JT knew if she did not put her foot down now, she would be a punching bag for the rest of her life. Shaking, she grabbed Ken's arm. "Ken, you are my date, and I would like to go back inside. So I'd really appreciate it if you would come with me!"

The firmness in her voice shocked all three of them. Even Nadia was momentarily speechless. And to JT's amazement, Ken turned and looked at her. His not-very-intelligent eyes registered that he was aware of behaving badly.

"Okay," he grumbled. "Let's go in."

JT smiled. Victory for once. She knew that Ken would rather stay out with Nadia, but that didn't matter. He was not important. What was going on here involved only her and Nadia.

JT and Ken began the slow march up the sand. But Nadia had one more trick in her pocket.

"Ken!" she sang.

When JT turned around, she could not believe what she saw. Ten feet away, lit only by the dim moonlight, stood Nadia Lawrence pulling her filmy white dress up over her head and letting it float down to the sand. There she stood, posed like a pinup, her perfect body clad in only a pair of pink lace underpants.

Nadia folded her arms over her breasts. "I'm

going for a swim." She giggled. "Anybody else want to come?"

JT had never seen anyone react as quickly as Ken did to that invitation. She barely saw him throw off his shirt, shorts, and shoes before they landed next to her in a heap and he was racing toward the water, wearing nothing but a pair of dark bikini briefs.

There was a huge splash and giggles and Ken's stupid voice telling Nadia he was going to get her. JT couldn't watch anymore.

Nadia had done it again. The fist had now ballooned inside until JT felt it in her head, her stomach, her back. Her whole body was throbbing with humiliation and rage. She ran, as fast and as far as her pale legs would take her. And when she finally felt she was out of Nadia's sight, JT fell on the sand and began to sob.

One other person, still back near the house, had witnessed Nadia's little scene—someone who had been watching, waiting, hoping for just this kind of opportunity

Quietly, with confidence and a sly grin, Elena Santiago walked down to the water's edge, picked up Nadia's white cotton dress, and carried it off.

❀ 14

NADIA HATED SWIMMING AT NIGHT. EVEN IN A SWIMMING pool she didn't like not being able to see the bottom. But in the ocean. Ughhh! Slimy things brushed past her legs, and when her foot touched bottom, she felt something shapeless and gooey. A jellyfish. Nadia was sure it was a jellyfish.

"There you are! Whoah, am I gonna get you!" called Ken.

Nadia could see the surf parting before his strong, purposeful strokes. She was shivering, but she swam hard and fast.

"That's what you think," she muttered, kicking up a fountain of water. Nadia's mission was accomplished. Ken was the perfect tool to prove to JT how she couldn't compete ... how much better off she'd be if she'd give up and join

Nadia's team again. But now that she had lured Ken away, Nadia wanted nothing more to do with him.

Suddenly a circle of bubbles rose right next to Nadia, and Ken shot up from under the water. Nadia wasn't sure how he'd reached her so quickly.

"I found you." He grinned. His blond hair was plastered down by the water, and a piece of seaweed was draped on his muscular shoulder. Nadia thought he looked like some moronic sea monster.

"You sure did," she responded nastily. "Now get lost." Then she slapped her hand along the water, splashing him right in his dumb, lecherous face.

"Hey!" Treading water, Ken floated there, looking suddenly confused. Nadia started swimming to shore.

Where had JT found this guy? Nadia wanted to be as far away from this creep as possible. Sure, Ken was handsome, but Nadia had known from the start he was a lowlife. Right off she'd noticed his generic polo shirt and those K-Mart jogging shoes.

Suddenly something slick and sinewy wound around her bare back, and Nadia almost screamed. UUUUGGGHH! Who knew *what* was swimming around out there! It was too disgusting to even think about. She twisted and tried to flick it away, when she realized what it was: Ken's other arm was now winding its way around her naked stomach.

"Let go of me!" Nadia screamed. She was outraged. One of his hands was now creeping up her rib cage. She jerked, her elbow slammed against his chest, and under she went, gulping a mouthful of seawater. Gasping for air, Nadia surfaced and found the bottom with her feet. Arms crossed over her breasts, she fought the tide and tried to walk out.

"Oooh, you won't get away that easy." Ken leered. He was right behind her, climbing out of the surf like the Creature from the Black Lagoon.

Nadia saw him coming and started to run. But the water whacked against her shins and down she went, her knee plunging into the soft sand. Fast as the current, she felt Ken's heavy body flop into her back. Again his hands reached and groped. Nadia pried at them with all her might. He was like an octopus.

"Leave me alone!" she screeched.

The tone in her voice finally did it. His arms relaxed, giving her just enough time to scramble up onto the dry sand. Goose bumps covered her skin, and she was now very aware of needing her clothes back ... quick! Her arms were practically glued over her breasts. She went for her dress. But it wasn't where she thought she'd left it. Maybe she'd drifted downwind in the water. Nadia looked up at the houses to figure out exactly where she was along the beach. That moment of hesitation was all Ken needed to catch up to her.

He grabbed her greedily, knocking her over.

Before she could prevent it, he was lying almost on top of her, his torso like a huge paperweight, his hot breath panting along the side of her neck. "You are such a little tease, aren't you?" he moaned. His voice had this awful raspy quality to it.

"I'm not teasing," Nadia growled. "Get off me." He tried to kiss her, and she violently turned her head, getting a mouthful of sand. Nadia spat it out. "I'M NOT KIDDING!" Ken continued to laugh . . . and grab. He was nibbling her ear like she was some kind of cabbage. Livid and desperate, Nadia directed her energy to her right knee. With all her strength, she lifted it and gave him a hard, swift kick.

"OOOOUUU!!!" he yelped, grabbing himself. He rolled off onto his back.

Nadia scurried to her feet. She looked for her dress. Where was that stupid dress!!

"What'd you do that for?" Ken asked, sitting up. His voice was full of surprise.

Nadia was still wildly searching for her clothes. "I just wanted to go for a swim. I didn't ask to be mauled!"

Ken slowly stood up. "You didn't? Well, that's news to me."

Nadia spotted a sloppy pile that she instantly recognized as Ken's generic polo shirt, khaki shorts, and K-Mart shoes. But he had left his clothes only a few feet away from where she'd dropped hers.

So where was her dress?!! She looked around in a panic, her teeth starting to chatter.

"What is your problem?" Ken demanded. "You only flirt like crazy and then take your clothes off. What'd you think you were doing? Inviting me to a picnic?"

Nadia had to get rid of this jerk. And she'd just noticed two couples walking along the beach up near the houses. Thank God she was in the dark. SHE HAD TO FIND HER DRESS!

"I was just swimming the way they do in France, in St. Tropez," she spat out. "That's all." She didn't know why she was bothering to explain.

"What?"

"You're too uncouth to know about things like that."

He put his hands on his hips and glared.

Nadia couldn't bother with him any longer. "Where's my dress?"

"How the heck should I know?" Ken angrily stomped over to his stack of clothes.

As Nadia watched the two couples stroll nearer, it dawned on her that her dress was gone, truly gone. Either it had been washed into the sea or someone had taken it. Whatever, she was standing on the middle of Malibu Beach practically stark naked! As Ken reached for his shirt, she rushed over and tried to grab it out of his hands.

He raised the polo shirt beyond her reach. Immediately Nadia brought her hands back down to cover herself.

"Ken," she said with forced sweetness.

He held his shirt under one arm as he pulled his shorts on over his wet underwear. "What?"

"Can I borrow your shirt? Please? It doesn't matter if you go back in just your pants, but me"—she giggled lamely—"I'll send it back to you later. Honest. Please. Come on."

A cruel smile came over Ken's face. Purposefully he took the knit shirt and pulled it on. "Sorry, baby." He grinned as his head popped through the neckline. "Looks like you're on your own." He grabbed his shoes and started up the sand.

"Ken!" Nadia ordered. The sheer terror in her voice made him turn back. "You can't leave me here like this! Come back here and give me that shirt!"

Ken waved. "Bye-bye. Tell JT I decided to split. Have a nice night."

Nadia could still hear him laughing as she skulked down to the water's edge and tried to figure out what in the world she was going to do.

About a quarter of a mile from where Nadia stood shivering, Amy Parker strolled along the shore, gazing at the crescent-shaped moon and the mesmerizing waves. Her thoughts were as jumbled as that churning water. The endless black made her feel even more unfinished, off-center, incomplete.

Was Cole making her suffer like this intentionally? Maybe he would show up at the very last minute, glad to have made her worry and wait. She looked back up the beach toward the house. All that light and noise just made her feel more unsettled.

But when she heard a halting cry, almost like the hoot of a wounded animal, she stopped and looked for its source. Something about the sound was so painful, so deep, that it knocked her own misery out of her head and filled her with concern for whoever was weeping.

Finally she saw it. A dark, huddled figure farther down the shore, about ten feet from the waterline. From where Amy was standing, she couldn't tell if it was a man, a woman, or what. Jogging closer, she saw it was a girl about her age in a light sleeveless dress. The girl was so hunched over that Amy couldn't see her face.

Amy put her hand on the girl's back, which was trembling from the force of her sobs.

"What's the matter?" Amy breathed, crouching down next to her. Her natural sympathy took over, and she slid an arm around the poor girl's shoulder.

The girl looked up, and Amy recognized her. She had met JT briefly at the party, although this bleary-eyed, red-faced creature was barely recognizable as the soft, pretty blonde Amy'd spoken to inside.

"She did it to me again," JT seemed to be saying, in between sniffs and gasps for air.

"Did what?" Anxious to comfort her, Amy rested

Linda A. Cooney

her cheek on JT's back. As she held JT, feeling the violent shaking, hearing the terrible cries, she thought back to Cole's pain the night before. Why was she so able to comfort this girl she barely knew, while she'd been unable to get through to Cole, a boy she might have loved? Why had she let him send her away like that, without an ending, not even a proper farewell?

Finally JT began to respond to Amy's comfort and calm down. She was too distraught to be embarrassed. When her crying stopped, she stared at the water with a limp, drained expression.

"Who did what to you?" Amy asked. She now sat at JT's side, just their shoulders touching.

JT shook her head and wiped her eyes with the back of her hand. "She used to be my best friend. But she just took away the guy I was with." The crying began again, but it was much milder now.

"Did you really like him?"

Now JT burst with something that was almost a laugh and a cry combined. "No! I couldn't stand him! But it just keeps happening to me. It's just like Denis all over."

"Denis?"

"I loved him, but he didn't love me. He never even called me before he left. It was all my fault that he drove so fast and ... I think I made him want to kill himself. I think I did."

JT rambled on about Denis and Nadia and a guy named Ken. Amy nodded and made sympathetic noises, but she was no longer really listening. Her imagination was starting to go crazy. The more she looked out at the rhythmic waves, the more she listened to JT's unhappy voice talking about Denis, the more a tiny seed of fear gnawed at her insides.

Kristin had told her all about Denis Daniels. And there was more to it than JT knew. Denis had fallen in love with Kristin, and when she told him she could not return his feelings, that was what prompted his life-threatening ride

As JT grew calmer, Amy became more and more agitated. Cole. Was Cole like Denis? Could that be the end of this stormy romance? Cole was the most emotional boy Amy had ever met, and she had just rejected him, returned his ring. When she left him last night, he looked as though he might be capable of doing anything. Would he react as Denis had?

She hadn't been able to reach Cole all day. Probably he was at the studio, but why couldn't she reach him tonight? Why wasn't he answering the phone? Amy began to feel clammy and sick. The rocking of the waves seemed incredibly ominous, and she had a terrible vision. Cole, on his white couch, the pillows billowing about him, his face pale and ...

Amy gasped out loud.

JT had stopped talking and turned to her. Her eyes were swollen, but she looked at Amy with affection. "Are *you* all right?" she asked sweetly.

Amy tried to swallow. "I just . . . I guess hearing about your friend, it made me think of somebody." Terrified, she stood up. "I have to go back in. Will you be okay?"

JT stood up, too, and shook the sand from her dress. "I'm okay. I guess I'll go back in, too. I just hope Nadia still isn't there."

Amy was glad JT was with her as they trudged back toward the house. She needed some support, and she had a sense, now that she was overwhelmed with worry, that JT would return her sympathy twofold. Amy walked faster and faster, the friction of the sand making her calves ache. But she barely felt it. The closer she got to that happy party house, the worse her premonition became.

If Cole had done something drastic, she was probably already too late. Not only that, the whole thing was completely her fault.

❀ 15

THERE ARE NO TREES ON A BEACH AND NO HEDGES. NOT even a bush or a bramble. That fact had never struck Nadia before. But never before had she crept along the Malibu shore praying for something, anything, to hide her humiliating nakedness.

She had gone over it in her head a million times. How could she get from the beach to her car without being seen? The path was blocked by houses, and suddenly every single one seemed to be sparkling with lamps and porch lights. Besides, what was she going to do when she got to her car? Of all nights, she had picked tonight to detach her convertible's top and leave it at home in the garage. She could just see it. Nadia Lawrence driving topless for the entire fifteen miles back to Beverly Hills! Nadia dug her nails into her palms. It was all she could do to keep from screaming.

Bent like an old woman, arms wrapped tightly around her chest, Nadia continued to pace along the water's edge. Only a few minutes ago some man had jogged up, and she'd had to duck into the ocean again to avoid being seen. Luckily, he'd been running fast enough so she hadn't been forced to wade too far out where all those creepy, slimy, disgusting things swim around. Uuuuggghhh! It was all too horrible!

Nadia crept further. Her heart jolted when she heard laughter. Oh, no! The thought of having to dive into that black water almost made her burst into tears. Then she spotted the source of the happy giggle and realized that neither of the pair would notice even if she leaped in front of them and danced the hula. Somehow that realization did not cheer her.

She saw Kristin and Grady stretched out on the sand. Even from where Nadia stood, she could hear happy whispers and that silvery laugh again. Oooh! It just made her more and more furious. Grady, that adorable, desirable Grady, making a fool of himself with that boring Minnesota twit while Nadia Lawrence skulked up and down the beach wearing nothing but a pair of drenched bikini underpants. Sometimes the world did not make sense.

Nadia started to slump down on the sand, when she made out a small mound not far from where

Kristin and Grady lay entangled. Could it be? *Please,* Nadia chanted in her head. Let it be a scrap, a rag, anything as long as it will cover my body. She suddenly thought of the hours she spent dressing, buying clothes, making sure she only put the right designer name on her back. Right now she'd be happy—ecstatic—over a housedress from Sears.

Creeping closer, she felt a rush of relief as the mound materialized as a folded towel. Thank God. At least it would cover her enough so that she could get away. Maybe there was still some justice left in the world.

As quietly and carefully as possible, Nadia stole over and, without interrupting Kristin and Grady, managed to snatch their extra beach towel.

By the time she reached the beach house, Amy was frantic. She was sure of the worst now. The suicide note, the method—it was all so terrifyingly vivid. She would never get over this. No matter what happened the entire rest of her life, this would always be the tragedy in her past that had left her unable to love again.

JT at her side, Amy stopped on the deck. The party was as festive and noisy as before, and Amy almost yelled out, "How can all you people be so happy when such a terrible thing has happened!" But she said nothing. Soon JT was called into the kitchen by Elena and, parting with a smile and thank-you, left. Amy was on her own.

Amy knew what she had to do. She would take Grady's jeep and go over to Cole's apartment. She would be the first one there, and she would take care of everything. Maybe, if she were very, very lucky, she would be in time to stop it.

Music still filled the living room, and although the dancing had stopped, the room was bursting with people. But where were Kristin and Grady? Amy surveyed every couch and corner. Almost hysterical, she forced her way through the crowd and into the entry hall. Someone took her arm.

Amy gasped.

"Amy."

That voice. Before she saw him, she let the voice settle inside her. That crisp, resonant, accented voice. Then she looked in his face. Cole was there, alive, standing right next to her. His skin was pink with good health, and his brown eyes were shining.

"Cole!" Amy cried. She threw her arms around his neck and pressed against him. She doubted she'd ever be so glad to see anyone ever again.

He responded with a funny sort of pat on her back. When she relaxed her grip to look in his face, he smiled.

"I was just going over to your house," Amy panted. She was so happy to see him she was almost crying.

"You were?" Cole was cool and casual. It was as if nothing out of the ordinary had happened.

"I was so worried about you."

"Worried?"

"Yes. I . . ." Amy stopped speaking. She had just noticed a girl standing next to Cole, a girl who was practically attached to his arm.

"This is Gail," Cole said, noticing Amy's interest.

Amy couldn't help staring. Gail was maybe a year or two older than Amy, with curly brown hair and wide, excited eyes. Amy was confused and could only think that this girl was Cole's sister or some friend from work.

"Hi, Gail," Amy said.

Gail smiled and with a blush snuggled her face against Cole's shoulder. Looking back at Gail, the actor grinned with an equally infatuated expression.

Amy was stunned. It took a moment for her to figure out quite what was going on. At first she thought this was some kind of act for her benefit, but when Cole looked at her again, she saw no malice in his eyes, nothing more complicated than easygoing friendship. Blank with confusion, Amy stared at them. Her brain was unable to compute this information.

Cole touched Gail's cheek. "Darling, I'll get you something to drink." He did not ask Amy if she wanted anything. "Be right back."

Gail watched him walk away down the hall. Then she faced Amy and exhaled heavily. Her cheeks were rosy, and she could not stop grinning. "You must be an old friend of Cole's," she heaved. Gail had this way of putting a lot of emphasis on one word that made her sound overdone. In that sentence she stressed the word "old."

"Sort of," Amy croaked.

"I don't mean to crash your party, but after what happened, I just *couldn't* refuse. And he *is* a big soap star."

"What do you mean ... after what happened?"

Gail leaned in as if telling a secret. "I was sitting in Alice's Restaurant all by myself, when this waiter comes over to me and hands me this note and this rose. I didn't know *what* was going on. And do you know what it said?"

Amy felt as though the blood were draining out of her body. "What?"

"It said that I was the most beautiful girl in the room and that he was waiting just for me. I look across the room, and there he is, Cole Stewart. *The* Cole Stewart. Then he took me for a drive to this place overlooking the beach. He didn't *say* anything. He stopped the car and kissed me. Just once. He is the most romantic guy I have ever met in my life. I am *so* in love."

Amy felt as if she were in a fun house—looking into one of those crazy mirrors that send back a distorted version of yourself. Her hand had even risen so that she was almost pointing at Gail. The corners of her mouth were quivering. She had no idea whether to laugh or cry.

Cole came back. He gallantly handed Gail her glass of soda and led her into the living room. As she watched Gail and Cole walk away, Amy almost stopped him and asked, Why? How could he do it? Didn't he even care for her?

But she didn't. She no longer feared she would burst into tears. Actually, in some crazy way, she felt the beginning of one of her famous giggling jags. After all, it was better to see Cole happy than lying on his white sofa covered by a sheet.

It was just so absurd! Amy had finally met someone who made her pull back—made her feel protective—only to discover that for Cole, being carried away was all he wanted.

Amy wandered back into the living room and sat on the edge of a crowded sofa. Suddenly everything she'd been through in the last week seemed ridiculous. Maybe going over the brink wasn't always such a good idea. Other people managed to get through life without falling into pigpens, having wild romances, and bashing up their knees.

She watched Cole and Gail walk down the hallway, arms around each other, both looking as if they'd found paradise. Amy suddenly found herself smiling. She just started to feel giddy . . . silly. It was like being at the dentist's office and getting laughing gas—she knew that it might hurt a little when the gas wore off, but at the moment all she could do was giggle.

Cole suddenly turned and looked her way. "Amy, is there anything the matter? You look rather peculiar."

Gail and Cole just stared as Amy began to laugh and laugh.

An hour later, Elena was having a good laugh of her own. "This is too good!" Elena yelled out loud. "JT! JT! Come over here, quick!"

JT stood on the other side of the living room, talking to Amy. Her eyes were still red, but amazingly, she'd stayed on at the party. Maybe it was only that she needed a ride home. Elena wasn't sure, but she preferred to believe JT was sticking it out just because she had guts.

JT and Amy squeezed their way over. They were smiling and chatting, looking as at ease with each other as two old friends.

"What is it?" JT asked. They joined Elena on the small sofa that sat under the living room window.

Elena bounced on the cushions and leaned toward the glass. She felt buoyant, as if she had won a major battle in a very long war.

With a huge breath, Elena pointed out the window. "Look!"

At first JT could not make out what she saw. Something was sneaking by, something with arms and legs, sopping hair, and a round bulky middle—it looked like a cross between a guerrilla commando and a giant bumblebee. Suddenly JT recognized the face and brought her hand to her mouth.

"It's Nadia." She gulped.

Immediately the three girls pressed up against the glass to stare.

And there she was. Nadia Lawrence, wrapped in a fat yellow-and-black beach towel, tiptoeing desperately past the house on her way to the street. The look on her face was one of pure misery.

Elena, the first to break away from the window, scooted down and pulled something white off the coffee table. Triumphant, she held up Nadia's dress.

"What do you think, girls? Should I send it to her marked Lost and Found?"

JT started to laugh. She wasn't so alone after all. "Sign the card 'with love.' "

Amy joined in, her out-of-control giggles returning. "How about '... thought you might have missed this!' "

All three fell onto the couch in a fit of laughter. Elena was pounding the cushions, Amy was holding her stomach, and JT was wiping the joyful tears from her cheeks.

Suddenly JT looked out the window again, and her giddiness ceased. For a moment she felt chillingly sober.

"Look, you guys." JT panicked.

Elena and Amy stopped laughing and sat up, too.

Nadia was standing right outside the window, staring in at them, her brown eyes huge with indignation and rage. Furiously clutching her towel, she looked as if she would like to destroy them with just the force of her gaze.

JT started to fold back down on the couch, but with Elena on one side and Amy on the other, there was nowhere to fall. Gathering support from her two friends, JT swallowed hard and leaned back against the window. She glared at Nadia. In the reflection of the glass, she saw Elena behind her, waving the dress like a flag of victory.

Nadia took a step toward the window and lifted an angry fist. For some reason, that made JT smile, and she waved her fingers. Taking their cue from JT, Amy and Elena began to wave, too.

"Hi, Nadia!" they all yelled in unison.

That did it. Looking so distraught that JT felt sorry for her, Nadia whipped around and ran off toward the street.

❀ 16

JT WOKE UP EARLY. SHE HADN'T FALLEN ASLEEP TILL after one, and all night she'd dreamed of storms and thunder. Now, as she pulled open her curtains and peered out into the backyard, she saw that it really was raining. The sky was dark, and the swimming pool was pitted by droplets of water. Pulling the covers up, JT cranked her window open and breathed in the cool, soggy earth.

Part of her was relieved at the unusual summer rain—not because it broke up the monotony of California weather (as it did), not even because it ended the heat wave and put out the last of the desert fires. No, she had a much more personal reason for welcoming this unseasonable shower.

Today was the famous softball game—the weekly

contest attended by Kristin and Grady, Monica, Josh, Holly, Eddie, and the rest. And this Sunday JT was invited. Elena had asked her in a fit of generosity as they sat laughing over Nadia's mishap. When JT had received the invitation two nights ago, she had swelled with pride. But as the game grew closer, JT had gotten more and more anxious. The Sunday softball games were the core of that group's togetherness. JT was not athletic. She barely knew the rules of the game. Besides, she still wasn't sure they would really want her there. Maybe it was raining just so she'd have a good excuse not to show up.

JT dragged herself out of bed and slipped out the door that led to the back patio. Huddled in a lawn chair under the redwood eaves, she watched the rain run through the ivy and the strawberry plants, leaving puddles at the base of her father's rosebushes. Her feet were cold, and she tucked them underneath her body, pulling her thin cotton nighty down to cover her knees.

She felt as though she were in some kind of space warp. She had truly broken from Nadia. There was no going back now. And yet JT still was not quite confident enough to join Elena and her friends. They kept welcoming her with open arms, but she didn't trust it. Too many times she had given of herself only to have the person she cared about reject and humiliate her. She was still too skittish and scared to jump into anything new.

For a long time JT sat outside, staring at the wooden fence, the rock clusters around the pool, the rain. A little before nine she heard the screen door slide open, and her mother padded out to join her. Her mom, so overweight she was practically bursting out of her colorful housedress, looked optimistic and jolly.

"Here you are." Mrs. Gantner smiled at the cloudy sky. "I love a summer rain," she said.

JT smiled, too. The warmth in her mom's face was hard to ignore.

In no hurry, Mrs. Gantner held out her hand to feel the water, then bent over to sniff a flowerpot of fresh herbs, finally coming up and smiling at her daughter again. "Somebody's on the phone for you."

"Me?"

Her mom nodded. "You can take it out here if you want." Still appreciating the wet morning, Mrs. Gantner plugged the telephone into the metal-covered outdoor outlet and delivered it to JT.

"Thanks."

Mrs. Gantner ruffled JT's hair, sniffed the herbs again, and wandered back inside.

JT stared at the telephone as if she'd never seen one before. Who could be calling her on a Sunday morning? Maybe it was Elena, phoning to say the game was canceled. Or was it Nadia finally calling to rub in her success with Ken and threaten JT with revenge for the disappearance of her dress? JT almost hung the phone back up.

"Come on. You can take it," she told herself. She could. No matter how Nadia taunted or jabbed, all JT had to do was think back to the look on her face as she rushed by that window, wrapped in that ridiculous towel. JT could handle Nadia.

Sitting up straight, JT put the receiver to her ear.

"Hello," she said firmly.

There was a short silence, and for a moment, JT thought the other party had hung up.

"JT?" It was a boy, but the connection was too fuzzy to place the voice.

"This is JT. Who's this?"

"This is Denis."

JT curled over the telephone. It was as though her body had melted away. In that instant all that was left of her was an ear, a mouth, and a far-off voice. Nothing else existed. No rain, no lawn chair, no swimming pool, nothing. Only Denis. Denis.

JT cradled the phone with both hands. "Where are you? Are you home?"

"No. I'm in Hawaii. It's about six in the morning here. What time is it there?"

His voice sounded different. Nervous. JT had never heard Denis sound nervous. "I guess it's around nine." It was an odd way to start the conversation, as if he'd called only to find out what time it was.

"Yeah. I got up early to help fix one of the cars here. It's sort of a point system. You do something extra, you get some kind of privilege. That's how come I got to call you."

"Oh." JT touched her lips to the receiver. It sounded as though Denis was in reform school. She found it impossible to picture beautiful, wild Denis buckling under to point systems and rules.

"Did you know I was here?" Again his voice had that anxious quality. He was talking a little too fast and without his usual carefree humor.

"I heard."

"Yeah."

The conversation ceased. JT held the phone even more tightly against her ear. She had to hear his voice again. "Denis, are you okay? Is it all right, that place?"

"Sure. It's okay," he came back with too much force.

JT knew he hated it. "Will you be at Sunset in the fall?"

"I don't know. I might want to stay here. You know, be the surf king of Waikiki."

That was the first time Denis's voice sounded the way JT remembered it: cocky, quick, sad.

"I miss you," JT said. The words came out before JT planned to say them. Just having those words on her lips released something inside. Her eyes welled up.

"Yeah. Uh, listen ..." He didn't finish. That edginess was back in his voice.

"Yes?"

"I, uh, I called to tell you something."

"You did?"

"Uh, I called for a reason, I mean."

"Oh."

"Yeah. See, I've been thinking a lot about the crash and what happened, and you and me. A lot. I've been thinking about it a lot."

The tears brimmed over and flowed down JT's cheeks as if they came from some disconnected place. She didn't tremble or sob, but still the tears ran. "Me, too."

"I just want to say it was my fault," Denis explained quickly. "I guess we didn't quite understand each other, but I always cared a lot about you, and I never wanted to hurt you, or get you hurt like that. What I mean is, I'm sorry. Oh, God, I'm so sorry."

JT held the phone against her cheek as if it were a wounded animal. The tears continued to wash down her face, but it was a good kind of crying, as if her insides were being cleansed.

"JT ... JT, are you still there?"

"Yes. I'm sorry, too, Denis."

"No. Don't apologize to me. You don't ever have to apologize to me."

Now there was a funny pull in his voice, and JT wondered if he was crying, too.

"Anyway, that's why I called. I can't stay on much longer. I didn't get that many points." He tried to laugh.

JT tried to laugh with him. "I'm so glad you

called." She heard a voice in the background telling Denis that his time was up.

"Guess I gotta go. Maybe I'll see you soon."

"I hope so."

"Yeah. Well, 'bye."

" 'Bye, Denis."

"Say hi to everybody."

"I will. See you soon."

"Yeah. Maybe. 'Bye."

He hung up.

"Good-bye," JT whispered again as she dropped the phone onto her lap. "Thank you."

JT sat in that lawn chair and let the tears keep coming until, of their own accord, they stopped. Suddenly she was more aware than ever of her body. She lifted her face, and the energy came surging back. Her legs felt springy and strong, her lungs were greedy for air, and her eyes were wide and clear.

When JT stood up to go back inside, it was still raining, although much more lightly. The pool gurgled, the flowers seemed to be drinking thirstily, and JT decided that the whole world looked just a little bit brighter.

She wasn't sure if people played softball in this kind of weather. But rain or shine, game or no game, she knew who the first person at that softball diamond was going to be. Janet Terry Gantner.

✻ 17

"THE BEST PART WAS WHEN AMY FINALLY CAUGHT A BALL, and then she fell in the mud."

"No, Kristin. I think JT was the best. She deserves a medal for her heroic slide into second base."

"Elena, I don't even know what a slide is. I just slipped."

"I loved it when the ball went into that puddle and we spent ten minutes trying to find it."

"Don't knock it, Amy. That was the only time our team scored a run."

All four girls laughed. Outside it was raining for the second straight day, but inside the Sullivan living room it was warm and cozy and smelled of popcorn. Amy was leaving later that afternoon, and the others were gathered for an informal good-bye.

Elena was lounging on the sofa, her feet resting on the antique coal bin. "What I couldn't believe was that Eddie asked that creepy David Michaels to play yesterday. He didn't even ask me first. And then Eddie puts me and David on the same team!"

Amy sat cross-legged on the rocking chair, stuffing herself with popcorn. "I thought it was kind of funny when you and David smashed into each other trying to get that fly ball."

Kristin nodded. She was on the floor, her long legs under the coffee table, the popcorn right in front of her. "Me, too. I loved it when he fell on top of you."

Elena looked indignant. "I think he did that on purpose!"

At the same time Amy and Kristin put their hands over their mouths. *"Nooooo,"* they cried sarcastically.

"What's that supposed to mean?"

JT piped up. She was perched on the armrest, her soft arms wrapped around her knees. "I think he's kind of interested in you, Elena," she said earnestly.

Elena rolled her eyes. "Yeah, yeah. He's interested in just how crazy he can drive me, that's what he's interested in. At work last night he tried to throw me into the whirlpool with all my clothes on."

"Ooooh." Kristin laughed. "Maybe next time he'll try it with your clothes off."

Elena put her hands on her hips. "Yuuck, spare me! More likely, he'll stick a whoopie cushion under my exercise mat. He is such a jerk!"

"Well," said Amy, laughing, "you know what they say...."

"What?"

"The lady doth protest too much."

Elena made a face. "Who said that?"

Amy shrugged. "I'm not sure. Hamlet, I think. Somebody in one of those Shakespeare plays I read this year."

"What's it supposed to mean?"

"You know," Amy told Elena. "Maybe you hate David so much because you don't really hate him."

"Or maybe I hate him so much because I really do hate him."

"Hey, Amy," objected Kristin. "I wouldn't bring Shakespeare into this. Look where *Romeo and Juliet* got you."

Amy fell forward and buried her face. "Don't remind me." She suddenly remembered something. "Hey, wait. What time is it?"

"A little after one-thirty," answered JT.

Amy held up her hands. "Quick, turn on the TV. Monica's on. And you-know-who."

Kristin scrambled up, opened the wood console, and flicked on the TV. Sure enough, there was Monica, looking like a lost waif. She was on her knees pleading with some silver-haired man.

All of them leaned forward. No one spoke as they watched their friend emote.

In the middle of a dramatic pause, JT whispered, "Um, what's going on? I've never watched this before."

Amy did not take her eyes off the set. "See Monica—her name is Sharon on the show—anyway, Sharon is really that guy's long-lost daughter, but he doesn't want to admit it."

"Really?"

"Really."

The music swelled, and the scene shifted. Now beautiful Felicia is opening the door to her apartment and, thinking she is alone, puts down her groceries ... but she's not alone. There is a young man on the sofa waiting for her.

"Ahhhh," Amy screamed, pounding the arms of the rocker. "It's him! The weirdest guy Amy Parker has come up with yet!"

They all gathered closer to watch Cole. He was now draped on the couch, holding Felicia's arm and begging for her to renew their romance.

"You know something," Amy said flatly, "that's exactly what he did with me. No wonder he was so good at it. He's had so much practice."

Kristin laughed. "I wonder if he's asked Gail to move in with him yet."

Amy fell back as if she'd just been shot. "Don't be cruel." She started to laugh. "I do think he gave her that ring, though. Oh, I can just see it. Gail, darling, I bought this ring just for you because the diamond reminds me of your eyes."

"You're taking it so well," JT said admiringly. "I don't know what I'd do if that happened to me."

"What can I do?" Amy grinned. "Besides, it was an adventure. And I got a great article out of it. It's going to be called 'Portrait of an Actor: Soap Opera versus Real Life.' Anyway, the best part of being out here was seeing Legs and meeting you guys. And that's not over."

JT and Elena shook their heads.

"I'll write," JT assured her.

"Me, too."

Amy turned away from the TV and looked at them. "You'd better. Maybe someday you'll all come visit me. I know St. Cloud is on the top of all your vacation lists."

Kristin looked a little teary. "It's on the top of mine."

They grew silent. A floor wax commercial was now on the screen, and they all looked at it. Clearly no one was really watching; rather they were thinking how much they didn't want Amy to leave.

"We'll miss you on the softball team," Elena finally said. "You're the only one who throws worse than Monica."

"I don't know," Kristin added. "After that slide, I think JT will fill Amy's slot just perfectly."

JT looked around with wonder, her round face full of hope. "Do you really think I should come next week and play again?"

Kristin smiled. "We may not be good, but we're persistent. Of course you have to come again."

JT blushed with pleasure. "Thanks. I guess I will."

They sat and watched the rest of the show, but neither Cole nor Monica reappeared. As the final credits rolled, Amy stood up, stretching her arms to the ceiling.

"Well, folks, I hate to say it, but it's time to go. If I miss my plane, my father'll think I ran off with some guy to Mexico or something."

They all stood up to get ready to go.

"Is it still raining?" Kristin asked.

Elena scooted into the kitchen to look out the window. "Yup. It's still coming down."

"I hope the station wagon makes it. It's been pretty funky ever since we drove it to the Renaissance Fair."

JT lingered in the hallway. "I can drive," she volunteered. "My Honda's just outside."

"Great," said Kristin. "We'd better get going."

They piled into JT's silver sedan, Amy and Kristin in the back, Elena up front with JT. It took about forty minutes to get to the airport. The whole time, Kristin reminisced about St. Cloud, Amy laughed over her adventure with Cole, Elena made fun of David Michaels—and JT Gantner sat quietly driving, her round face the picture of contentment and pride.

Here's a sneak preview from WORKING IT OUT, the sixth book in the "Sunset High" series for GIRLS ONLY.

"IT'S TRUE," ELENA INSISTED. "WHEN I'M AROUND DAVID Michaels I think I need a guy like a fish needs a bicycle."

"Like a dog needs a microwave," Monica laughed.

"Like a tree needs a skateboard," added Kristin.

"Like a bird needs a garbage disposal," topped JT.

Grady stood up and hiked up his swim trunks. "Come on, Josh," he urged. "We'd better go in the water before they lynch us."

With a nod of his curly head, Josh stowed his glasses and stood up too. "You're telling me."

Feeling cocky and strong again, Elena unfolded her long trim legs and joined them. "I'll race you down to the water, gentlemen. Last one in is an inferior species."

Grady, Josh, and Elena looked at one another and began to run. Like hurdlers they leaped over ice chests, sleeping bodies, striped backrests, and sand castles till they were crashing into the waves. Both boys were muscular and fast, but lean, leggy Elena made it there first.

The girls still on the sand formed a circle and faced one another.

"What do you think?" JT said softly, tugging on her single long earring.

Monica pulled her legs up underneath her and gave a dramatic sigh. "About Elena and David?"

JT nodded.

"I'll tell you what I think," asserted Kristin. She was looking at the water with her level, straight forward gaze.

"What?"

"She's absolutely crazy about him."

ABOUT THE AUTHOR

Linda A. Cooney grew up in Southern California and has worked as an actress in both New York and Los Angeles. In addition to creating the SUNSET HIGH series, she has written five other popular young adult novels. She lives in New York City.